"Fine. W
No questions. No promises.
No problems. And you can reserve
the right to change your mind
if you feel the need. But—"

He cut her off with a kiss so potent it left her
breathless. His tongue was almost acrobatic in its
mission. It twirled and flipped and spun in her
mouth as if it were the star attraction in the greatest
show on earth.

She couldn't be outdone so early in the game, so she
moved her tongue slowly in and out of his mouth,
interrupting his pace, slowing it down but keeping
the heat of the kiss. She arched her back and moved
her hips, swiveling them and rocking them against
the hard press of his masculinity.

He let her slide down off the wall. His eyes were
hooded in desire as he gazed at her. He lifted the
hem of her sundress, his hand inching up her thigh
in a slow seductive manner until he reached the part
of her inner thigh closest to her core.

"Just relax and enjoy the ride," he whispered.

Books by Gwyneth Bolton

Kimani Romance

If Only You Knew
Protect and Serve
Make It Hot
The Law of Desire
Sizzling Seduction
Make It Last Forever
Rivals in Paradise

GWYNETH BOLTON

was born and raised in Paterson, New Jersey. She currently lives in central New York with her husband, Cedric. When she was twelve years old, she became an avid reader of romance by sneaking books from her mother's stash of Harlequin and Silhouette novels. In the '90s she was introduced to African-American and multicultural romance novels and her life hasn't been the same since. She has a B.A. and an M.A. in English/creative writing and a Ph.D. in English/composition and rhetoric. She teaches college-level classes in writing and women's studies. She has won several awards for her romance novels, including five Emma Awards and a *Romance in Color* Reviewers' Choice Award for new author of the year.

When Gwyneth is not teaching or working on her own romance novels, she is curled up with a cup of herbal tea, a warm quilt and a good book. She can be reached via email at gwynethbolton@prodigy.net. And readers can visit her website at www.gwynethbolton.com.

RIVALS in PARADISE

Gwyneth Bolton

KIMANI™
ROMANCE

This novel is dedicated to all my *sistah*-authors, for writing the amazing books that keep the genre of Black Romance alive. Nikki Giovanni told us that black love is black wealth and I know it's true every time I read your books. Keep on writing and making this a genre that I am so proud to be a part of....

 KIMANI PRESS™

ISBN-13: 978-0-373-86186-6

Recycling programs for this product may not exist in your area.

RIVALS IN PARADISE

www.kimanipress.com

Printed in U.S.A.

Dear Reader,

There is something about the rivals-to-lovers story that *never* gets old for me. Most of my favorite television couples have some element of rivals to lovers in their stories.

Who can forget *A Different World,* when Dwayne Wayne and Whitley Gilbert traded barbs in the early days of the show when he thought he was head over heels in love with Denise Huxtable? We all know how that turned out— with the famous wedding-crasher show and Dwayne begging… "Whitley, I love you! Please, baby, please!"

And then there is my all-time favorite couple, Maxine Shaw and Kyle Barker from *Living Single.* They took the "I hate you! I love you!" push and pull of rivals to lovers to passionate new heights.

These couples made crossing that thin line between love and hate oh so much fun! And if you enjoy journeys to love that are just a little vexed but also a whole lot of fun, then you are going to enjoy Cicely "Cee Cee" Stevens and Chase "The Wolf" Yearwood's trip down love's rocky road immensely.

From the minute Cicely stepped on the scene in *If Only You Knew,* I knew she'd have a wonderful story to tell one day. This younger sister was spicy and sassy and I knew I had to find just the right hero for her. It took me a minute, but I found him. You're going to love Chase. He's smooth, funny, 100 percent alpha male, every bit of fine and he loves Cicely to distraction (even if it takes him a minute to realize it). I hope you enjoy Cicely and Chase's story. Be sure to look for my April 2011 release, *At First Kiss!*

Much love and peace,

Gwyneth

Acknowledgments

I want to acknowledge my family, because without their support I wouldn't know what love is or be able to write about it. Special thanks to my husband, Cedric Bolton, my mom, Donna Pough, my sisters, Jennifer, Cassandra, Michelle and Tashina, my nieces Ashlee and Zaria and my nephew Michael.

To all the readers, thanks so much for all your emails and notes. Hearing from all you smart and savvy readers always makes my day!

Thanks to all the book clubs who have read my novels, especially SistahFriend, Sexy Ebony BBW African American Book Club, Sistas' Thoughts from Coast to Coast and the Prominent Women of Color Book Club.

I also want to thank the ladies of the Live, Love, Laugh and Books Yahoo Group. The readers, writers and aspiring writers in this group, along with my fellow host authors—Shelia Goss, Michelle Monkou and Celeste Norfleet—are one amazing group of people.

Finally, I want to send an extra-special dose of love and appreciation to the Shelfari Black Romance Reading Group. I have so much fun talking about black romance novels with you all. I'm sure my local bookstore thanks you, too, because we are all so willing to enable each other's book-buying addictions!

Chapter 1

"**O**hmygodohmygodohmygod. Oh. My. *God!*
Harder. Harder. Harder!"

Cicely "Cee Cee" Stevens walked toward the
master bedroom of her condo with her eyes and mouth
wide open. There was no way she could possibly be
hearing what she thought she was hearing.

Not in her house.

Not in her bedroom.

No damn way was this happening to her after the
day she'd just had at work!

But the squeaking of the bedsprings and the bang,
clunk, bang, clunk, bang of the headboard didn't lie.
Isaac was cheating on her....

That lowlife had another woman in her bedroom. In her bed! And he had better be thankful that she didn't own a firearm. The old adage that God protected babies and fools was obviously true, because if she'd had a gun...heaven help the fool!

At one time not all that long ago, Cicely's job had been all-important to her. She had known that she was damn good at it. As an executive in the corporate finance department of the huge media firm Mainstay, she was well-known all across Miami for her business acumen and savvy. She'd had a style and flair for business that made money appear with such ease folks had hardly realized that money was moving.

Now, however, her new passive-aggressive, anal-retentive division leader, Leonard Stone, barely gave her breathing room, and the workplace had become a hostile environment.

Her new division leader had graduated from FAMU, as she had, and she'd tried on numerous occasions to build a better working relationship with the insufferable man. But he wouldn't budge, and she was starting to think that she might need to start pounding the pavement, looking for another position.

She'd had hopes of moving up the corporate ladder. She'd hoped to try her hand at corporate development so that she could work in mergers and acquisitions and really make deals, not just get the money to make

the deals happen. She'd thought she was a shoo-in
to get the division leader position in the corporate
development department when it opened up. But she
had no such luck.

The promotion should have been hers. It would
have gotten her away from the division leader from
hell and in charge of her own department. Instead,
she'd just found out, it was going to some interloper
who was more than likely a friend of Leonard
"The Evil One"—as she had grown fond of calling
him—Stone.

Home sweet home was usually her space of refuge,
a place to wind down and relax. But now she had
come home after a particularly hard day at work to
find her nice, quiet, nerdy, handpicked-because-he-
would-*never*-hurt-her boyfriend Isaac in the bed with
another woman.

Can a sista catch a break? Seriously?

He was supposed to be waiting for her so that they
could celebrate the promotion she'd thought was hers
when she came back from celebrating with her girls.
Thirty-year-old Cicely had just given the cheater a
key to her place after a year and a half of being a
couple. It seemed like the logical next step, since her
biological clock was ticking loudly. It was starting
to sound like a hurricane warning tone on full blast.
And he had seemed like the perfect candidate for a
future husband. Nice. Safe. Sweet. A little bookish...

okay, maybe totally nerdish…but sweet…definitely sweet…

And he wasn't supposed to hurt her like this!

She took a deep breath as she reached the door. His cheating just proved her original beliefs, the ones she'd had almost all her life… *No man is safe when it comes to matters of the heart.*

The only person who can protect your heart is you.

It's better not to fall in love.

She'd decided a long time ago that she would never get caught slipping and falling in love. But she did have deep feelings for Isaac, the kind of camaraderie they could have built a nice, strong, sturdy lifetime on…

She was certain that if she was really in love with Isaac, the lying, cheating, humping-another-woman-in-her-bed jerk, she wouldn't be able to open the door and calmly do what needed to be done.

That's why love was a problem. If she loved him she might have thought twice about kicking his faithless behind to the curb!

She opened the door and saw exactly what she thought she would see. Isaac was screwing some floozy.

She slammed the door behind her and cleared her throat.

The startled lovebirds broke apart, each grabbing for the cover.

Cicely frowned because she had purchased those 500-count ecru Egyptian cotton sheets just a few weeks ago and now she would have to burn them or at least throw them in the trash. Because there was no way in hell she would ever sleep on them again. She glanced around at her recently remodeled—so it wouldn't look so girlish and make the cheating boyfriend she had just given a key to uncomfortable—bedroom. Everything from the chocolate duvet to the ecru sheets would have to go.

"Sorry to interrupt. But since this is *my* bedroom in *my* condo and all…I'd appreciate it if you both get your nasty asses out. Now!" Cicely put one hand on her hip and pointed toward the door with the other.

Isaac grabbed his glasses off of the mahogany-and-nickel nightstand and the sheet dropped. The woman pulled more of the sheet over herself, and Cicely wondered when they were going to get their nasty behinds off of her platform bed.

Yuck. Just. Yuck. Would she have to get a new bed, too?

She rolled her eyes as Isaac struggled with the woman for the sheet and tried to explain himself at the same time.

"Baby, I can explain.… She means nothing to me.… It was just a one-night thing.… She's been throwing herself at me for months.… I'm just a man.… Baby, please…" Isaac's words started to jumble together as he leapt from the bed and pulled on his trousers.

Once the other woman resigned herself to getting out of the bed, she at least had the good taste to get dressed quickly and quietly. Cicely did notice that the woman cut Isaac more than a few nasty looks while he was rambling out his apologies and explanations.

The woman was pretty if you liked tall, slim model types with perfect chocolate skin, big doe eyes and cute, pixie-style haircuts. Once clothed, she wore a rather nice purple pantsuit and killer matching shoes. Cicely had to give it to Isaac; at least he picked a really attractive woman to cheat with.

The woman walked over to the bedroom door where Cicely was firmly posted. With her arms folded across her chest, Cicely gave the woman the once-over and, with one scathing look, dared her to say anything out of line.

The woman took a deep breath and bit her lip.

Cicely arched an eyebrow.

"Look. I don't want any trouble. He misrepresented his situation to me. And for what it's worth, I apologize for my part in this. I'd just like to leave now. I didn't mean you any harm, Cicely." She turned to Isaac and spat out, "You're a jerk!"

Shocked that the woman knew her name, Cicely gave her a more thorough once-over. She realized she knew the woman. She was the lobby receptionist in the office building that both she and Isaac worked in.

The accounting firm that Isaac worked for was on the ninth floor of the building, and the company Cicely worked for was on the fifteenth floor. Cicely couldn't help rolling her eyes then.

If Isaac and she had initially hooked up by meeting in the elevator of that building, then why not Isaac and the lobby girl? With so many other companies and employees located in the high-rise office building, who really knew how many other women this geek-nerd-jerk of a man had been with or was still sleeping with?

As if he could tell where she was going, Isaac began pleading his case again. "This was the first time. I have never… I would never, *ever* do something like this to you. You gotta believe me, baby. I love you.… I just started to get cold feet, that's all.… Things were starting to get real serious between us, with us exchanging keys and all…it's a big step…"

Both Cicely and the lobby woman sucked their teeth at the same time.

Cicely stared at the woman again.

Pam!

Her name was Pam. Cicely now remembered

that she had always thought that Pam's smiles and greetings were a bit false whenever the woman would say hello as she signed into the building in the morning.

Now she knew why.

Cicely stepped aside and let Pam leave. Hearing the front door close, Cicely turned her attention back to the cheater.

Isaac's usual toasted-cinnamon complexion was looking almost ruby-red. He ran his hand across his close-cropped hair several times. He always did that when he was thinking. Now Cicely thought it might be a sign that he was trying to think of a lie.

"I love you, Cicely. You gotta know that…" Isaac started. "I thought you were going out with your sister and girlfriends for happy hour?"

The mention of her canceled girls' night out celebration focused her attention on yet another reason why this had to be the worst night ever. After finding out that she had been passed over for the promotion, she'd called her two best friends and her sister to cancel their impromptu celebration. She'd felt like curling up on the sofa with some Chunky Monkey ice cream, her favorite torn sweatpants and FAMU T-shirt, a blanket and her boyfriend, feeling sorry for herself.

Is that really too much to ask for? Seriously?

Instead, she came home to her boyfriend in her bed with another woman.

Isaac reached out and touched her shoulder, trying to pull her closer to him.

"Uh-uh. No. Don't you ever touch me again! And I want you out of my condo. Give me your key and get the hell out. Take anything of yours here because you will never be coming back!" She turned and walked out of the master bedroom.

She couldn't stay in the condo tonight. Finding him in her bed with another woman had left her feeling almost violated. He had tarnished the sacred space of her home. She had to get out of there. At least for a little while.…

He followed her with his pants half-zipped. *Ironic.*

"Baby, please don't do this. Please don't go. Where are you going? Are you going to your sister's place?"

"It's none of your business where I'm going. And why are you still here? Give me my keys and get the hell out." She hissed out her words with all the venom she felt for him.

"I don't want to go. I don't want our relationship to end. Can't you give me another chance? Can't we work this out?" He gave her a pleading look and a nervous grin. "I made a mistake. But if you love me, we can get past this."

If she loved him…

She cared about him deeply. She had committed herself to building a life with him because he was supposed to be a safe bet. But she didn't love him in that way that always landed women in trouble unless they existed in some make-believe romance novel or chick flick where everything always turned out perfectly and everyone always lived happily ever after.

That's why she had thought she would be safe. She knew enough not to believe that fairy tales existed in the real world. That's why she'd picked Isaac. He wasn't the fairy-tale type, far from it. But he was her shot at a nice, staid, secure and somewhat happily-ever-after life.

Was this her fault for settling into a relationship she thought was safe?

She shook her head.

No.

This wasn't her fault.

It was his sorry, no-good, trifling fault. She went to her closet and started packing a bag. She was normally a nonviolent, peaceful person. But she had to get out of there before she caught a case.

Isaac reached out and touched her shoulder. She turned and glared at him, giving her eyes just enough squint to show that she meant business.

"If you want to keep that hand, I suggest you keep

it off of me. And get out!" Speaking through clenched teeth, she counted to ten in her head.

Woosah...Woosah...

He pulled his arm back quickly and she continued packing in silence.

She had no idea where she was going to go. She just knew she had to get the hell out of there. She thought about going to her sister, Latonya's, house. But then she'd have to put up with her older sister feeling like she had to fix things for her baby sister. And her brother-in-law, Carlton, would probably make it his business to put Isaac in his place.

And if she went to Gran's house, her grandmother would probably put a hurting on Isaac worse than anything Carlton or Latonya could ever do. Even in her eighties, Gran wasn't anyone to mess with and she didn't tolerate people messing over her girls.

No, it was best that she go to a hotel for the night. Yes, a luxury hotel with lots of amenities and a top-of-the-line snack bar to raid would be the perfect place for her to lick her wounds. She would pamper herself for the night, or maybe even the weekend, and come back as good as new to her now-defiled condo. She would be ready to face it then. Maybe buy some new sheets and a new duvet on the way home from the hotel.

I can do it, she told herself.

She pulled up the handle on her small rolling

suitcase, cut a sneer at the now sniveling idiot sitting on her bed and walked over to him with her hand out.

"Key, please."

He reached in his pants pocket and took her key off his key ring.

"Finish getting dressed and get to stepping."

She watched as he slowly finished dressing, then walked him to the door, barely resisting the urge to kick him in his backside as he exited her condo.

She waited for him to be good and gone before she exited, too. She didn't know where she was going, but she knew she was getting the hell out of there.

Chase "The Wolf" Yearwood took a sip of his drink after toasting to the good old days and brand-new beginnings with his college buddy, Leonard Stone. Chase's taking the job as the head of the corporate development division at Mainstay Media where Leonard was the head of the finance department was the reason for their little happy-hour celebration.

At thirty-three years old, Chase had made more than a name for himself in the business world. Chase had made his former employer lots of money by relying on his keen kill-or-be-killed instincts. His instincts helped him in his personal life as well, especially in his relationships with the opposite sex. His law-of-the-jungle approach to dealing with the selfish, money-grabbing women he had become used to reinforced his nickname of "The Wolf," in both the bedroom and the boardroom.

But in the boardroom, his former superiors had started to second-guess him and question his actions in unproductive ways. Chase refused to be stifled. So, he landed a sweet new position based on a tip from his old college buddy, Leonard Stone. He planned to start the new job just as soon as he took a trip to Dahinda, the island he'd been born on and the place he still called home.

His narrow focus on work and only work had caused him to miss the chance to be at his grandmother's bedside when she'd passed away. He felt more than a little guilty about missing her passing and missing the chance to tell her how much she had meant to him. He planned to use the trip home to reevaluate his priorities and reconnect with what was important. He wouldn't let work keep him away from the rest of his relatives, especially his mother, Margie.

The job at Mainstay was slightly different from Chase's former job. He would still be in charge of mergers and acquisitions. However, the "corporate raider" aspect of his former job would be missing. He would be more hands-on in development instead of swooping in and gobbling up struggling companies so that they could be taken apart and sold off piece by piece. He would be building things now.

"You're going to love it at Mainstay, Yearwood!" Leonard slapped him on the back and let out a chuckle.

Leonard hadn't changed all that much in the years since college. He was tall and still somewhat lanky. He had what some would call a swimmer's build. His formerly thick, wavy hair was now making a slow creep away from his forehead, but he hadn't gone the shave-it-all-off route that most men went when faced with balding. He had a weird comb-it-all-to-the-front thing going on that really did nothing to hide the fact that he was going bald. His hazel eyes were still astute and focused and didn't give anything away about the man behind them.

"And I'm going to love the fact that everyone knows I was instrumental in bringing you to Mainstay. It gave me major points with the boss, and as long as you do your thing the way you've done it in your previous job, I'm sure we'll both be moving on up to the vice president slots soon."

Chase squinted a little. He wasn't sure how he felt about Leonard lumping their possible future promotions together like that. He had always been a man who went by his own merit, played by his own rules and made his own way. When he'd pledged Omega as an undergraduate, he'd earned the line name "The Lone Wolf" because he'd pledged solo with no line brothers, just himself. He had been an only child. He always had been, and always would be, his own man.

He hadn't needed Leonard to get the job, and he certainly wasn't going to allow Leonard to ride his coattails to a promotion. Leonard telling him about the position was not equivalent to his hard work and preparation giving him the experience and tools he needed to get hired into the position. He didn't like at all what Leonard was insinuating.

But rather than spoil the celebratory mood, Chase just made a mental note to watch Leonard.

"It'll be great, man. Just like old times when we ran the student government at FAMU," Leonard added.

Chase frowned. "I'm looking forward to the new job and developing my strengths in other areas. The change will be nice, and it will keep me sharp, help me keep my edge."

"There aren't many men sharper than you, Yearwood, that's for sure. Aside from that unfortunate election for president of the student government back at FAMU, you've pretty much accomplished everything you ever went after." Leonard chuckled.

Chase felt the veins in his neck pulse just a little as he arched his left eyebrow.

Leonard laughed. "Hey, we all have to lose sometimes. You'd been on top all through undergrad. And you're making big moves all throughout the business world now. Who cares about something as insignificant as the student government race from our undergraduate days? Although…" Leonard opened his mouth and closed it.

Chase's nostrils flared. Now he knew Leonard was trying to start something with him. Everyone who knew him back in college and still had the privilege of being in his inner circle of associates knew he did *not* talk about the student government association election that took place at the end of his junior year.

Ever.

It wasn't just that he had lost the election.

It was so much more than that.

So. Much. More.

It was personal, very personal. And he didn't like anyone bringing it up.

Rather than tell off an old friend he was now going to have to work with, Chase opted to change the subject. "So, Leonard, what can you tell me about Mainstay and the day-to-day work environment?"

"Oh, I'm sure you'll find it interesting. In fact, I'm betting you'll find it more than interesting." Leonard took a swig of his beer. "With the two of us there now, having each other's back, it'll be a lot like old times. *A lot* like old times…"

"Our college days are over. We're grown men now. Those days are long behind us." Chase heard the slight edge in his own voice and wondered yet again if he was doing the wrong thing by joining a company where his old friend was also employed. Corporate politics could be complicated enough without bringing in the extra drama or building alliances before he even got a chance to learn the lay of the land.

Friend or no friend, Chase wasn't about to let Leonard pull him into any mess. "Well, I'm a quick study. I'm sure I'll be able to assess the situation once I start in two weeks."

"Must be nice to be able to take a vacation," Leonard said with a smirk.

Chase paused because he thought he detected a slight shade of snide and a small dose of snark in Leonard's voice.

"I haven't taken a proper vacation in so many years I almost don't remember what a vacation is, and I haven't been home to Dahinda for a visit in so long my mother has threatened on numerous occasions to disown me and find herself another son. I think two weeks on my home island is just what I need before starting a new job with a whole new set of demands."

Leonard rolled his eyes. "I'll hold down the fort until you come on board. Once you're there, I'll fill you in on all the dirt and all the stuff you *really* need to know. But for now, it's good to be working with you again, my friend."

Chase simply nodded and hoped that he wouldn't walk into Mainstay in two weeks and find that he had made a huge mistake by taking this job offer instead of one of the countless others that had been offered to him when the business world got wind that The Wolf was ready to make a move.

Cicely placed the pillow over her head and tried to block out the noise. Someone kept playing the same six bars of a song over and over again. It took her a couple of minutes to realize that it was her cell phone's ring tone that was disturbing her sleep.

She was at the Wyndham Hotel by Miami International Airport because that was the only hotel with a vacancy. The upcoming holiday and some teachers' convention had the other local hotels filled to capacity.

The singer's voice and the song that *used* to be one of her favorites blared out yet again, and Cicely grabbed the phone. If it was that cheating, no-good Isaac, she was going to lose the little bit of religion she had and give him the verbal blasting he so richly deserved.

"What?" Cicely snapped.

"Well, hello and good morning to you, too, Cee Cee."

Cicely sat up at the sound of her older sister's voice. This was the woman who had literally put her life on hold and made sacrifice after sacrifice so that Cicely could have all of the extras in life. Six years older than Cicely, Latonya had worked while she was in college to help keep a roof over their heads. Then she had literally covered everything that Cicely's scholarships didn't so that Cicely could attend FAMU and not have to worry about working. And when she had married a very rich and successful businessman, he had stepped in and helped take care of his new wife's little sister and grandmother to take the load off of his wife.

Although Latonya Stevens-Harrington would be the last person to expect any kind of gratitude for the things she'd done to help Cicely through the years, Cicely felt the weight of her indebtedness to her sister. She would never be able to repay Latonya for all that she had done for her.

However…all that indebtedness didn't take away from the fact that it was super early on a Saturday morning, and all Cicely wanted to do was sleep.

"Morning, Peanut." She called her older sister by her family nickname still, and she was probably the only person in the world that Latonya allowed to do so. "Can I call you back at a decent hour, say noon or so?" Cicely flopped back down on the bed and curled into the fluffy down comforter.

"Sorry, no can do. Gran and I have been calling you all morning. We were worried sick about you. Gran said she called your condo numerous times. I finally found Isaac's number and called him. He wasn't answering. Then I called his cell after I didn't get an answer on your cell. He said you broke up with him. He sounds horrible, by the way, really distraught. But you must have a good reason for breaking up with him, and I would never tell you to second-guess yourself. But do you want to talk about it at all? What happened? Why did the two of you break up so suddenly?"

"She should have left that guy a long time ago! I never liked him. She should let me introduce her to someone worthy." Carlton Harrington III's big booming voice could be heard in the background. He must have been sitting, or, knowing the two of them, lying down in the bed right next to Latonya.

Latonya shushed him.

Cicely stretched out her legs and curled them back up. "Tell my darling brother-in-law that, although I love him to death, the I-love-me-some-alpha-jerk-reformed-playboys gene skipped me. I can't fathom having anything in common with *anyone* he would introduce me to."

Latonya echoed Cicely word for word, and Carlton could be heard gruffly mumbling that his wife didn't have any complaints. There was more giggling from

Latonya, and Cicely didn't even want to think what Carlton must have been doing to her sister to warrant all those girlish giggles. It was *TMI* too dang early in the morning.

"That's cold, Cee Cee. I thought we were better than that," Carlton joked in the background.

"Smooches." Cicely made a kissing sound. "Now, if that's all, I really—"

"Oh, no, that's not all. Gran and I have been thinking of what we can do to lift your spirits since you just lost that promotion… And now with everything that is going on with Isaac… You still haven't told me exactly what happened, by the way…" Latonya let her words hang suggestively.

And I'm still not going to, at least not yet.

"Neither of which would be a problem if she would just come and work for Harrington Enterprise and let me hook her up with a real man instead of these Steve Urkel wannabes she keeps dating." Carlton added his two cents, clearly getting Cicely back for her previous dig.

"Carlton!" Latonya let out an exasperated sigh.

Cicely laughed. Even if she really thought she had hurt her brother-in-law's feelings with her comment about the alpha-jerk-reformed-playboys, she still would have laughed. Because rich, stunningly handsome control freaks like him needed to be taken down a peg whenever possible, and her sister was too crazy in love to do a proper job of it.

She knew she could have easily taken a job at her brother-in-law's company, Harrington Enterprise. But she was serious about making a mark on her own. She had her sister to thank for all the sacrifices she'd made to ensure that Cicely became the woman she was. But she drew the line at nepotism and relying on family connections to get ahead in the business world.

"Anyway, Cee Cee, Gran and I figured we'd take a little shopping trip to New York City. We haven't been to the penthouse there in forever, and the kids might even get to see some snow. You have the week off from work. It would be great. "

"Huh?"

"Thanksgiving in New York City. Macy's Parade. Kids happy. Your mind off of the stress in your life, *shopping* the Friday after Thanksgiving…*in New York City…*" Latonya let her words trail in an enticing manner.

Cicely thought about it. She truly loved her niece and nephews. Carlton IV was eleven and Terrence was eight. They looked like their father but had their mother's calm and loving personality. Her little niece, Evelyn "Evie" Harrington, was the spitting image of Latonya, but she had Carlton's over-the-top, sometimes overbearing personality. Cicely sometimes called her little niece the five-year-old terror. But she loved those kids. She loved the family her sister had been able to create. She just wondered when she was going to be able to start a family of her own.

She really wasn't in the holiday spirit. She would have been a killjoy for everyone. It was best if she stayed behind.

"Nah. You all can go without me. I'm not going." Cicely sat up.

She had pretty much decided that she was going to spend the week away from people she knew. She'd do some self-reflection. Maybe a little wallowing in self-pity—just a little…. Then she would pick herself up and put the pieces back together again.

She had already started to psychoanalyze herself, and she had pretty much decided that even though her daddy issues hadn't surfaced in the same ways as her older sister's had, and she'd always thought she didn't have any daddy issues at all, she clearly had them and then some to spare.

Gran, their father's mother, raised Cicely and Latonya after their own mother died. Their father had left the family years before that and never looked back. They didn't know if he was dead or alive now. Even with all the love their grandmother poured into them as she raised them on her limited resources, the telltale signs of little girls neglected by their father followed both women into adulthood.

Latonya's daddy issues had made her believe that love wasn't a possibility in her life. Even though she had married one of the richest men in the country, she spent the first part of their marriage waiting for the proverbial other shoe to drop, waiting for Carlton to get tired of her and leave. That's why when their marriage was tested by interference from Carlton's meddling grandfather, Latonya gave up without a fight. It took years for them to rebuild their marriage and learn to trust in their love.

Cicely didn't know if she trusted love or not. But she liked to think that she was wiser because she never chose men that could possibly break her heart the way her father did. Even though she was very young when her father turned his back on their family, she had vivid memories of his larger than life, ladies' man persona. What he lacked in money, he made up for in charisma. And whenever he was around, it hardly mattered what their mother wanted. He was the man. He ruled. Cicely made it her business to stay away from those kinds of men. She picked nice quiet guys because she couldn't trust men like her father to love her.

Daddy issues? Yes, she had them, too.

However, all she needed to do was spend the week digging into her psyche and hit the church after she'd done the heavy lifting in order to top off the self-therapy with some Jesus and she'd be fine. She was her grandmother's child, after all, and that side of the family didn't believe in paying for therapy when a little tough love and taking it to the Lord would do just fine. Isaac's betrayal had thrown her off track, but she could fix this and then she'd be good as new. That's why she really needed this time away.

"I'm sorry, Peanut, but I'm not going to spend Thanksgiving with the family this year. I'm not going to New York with you all."

"Now, Cee Cee, you know we have to celebrate Thanksgiving as a family. Gran is getting up in years, and who knows how much longer we'll have her around to celebrate the holidays with? We should be there for Gran if nothing else."

"Sorry, I have to pass this time, Peanut. With everything that happened since yesterday, I really can't be around people right now. I love you and Gran, but I need you guys to respect my wishes on this one...."

"Aww, come on, Cee Cee.... Please consider it...." Latonya's pleading voice was almost enough to make Cicely reconsider.

Latonya had spent three years away from the family when a misunderstanding caused Carlton to make her leave their home and their child. Latonya had been pregnant with their second child at the time and no one knew it. Those three years had made Latonya want to hold her family even closer once she came back. Usually, Cicely was willing to indulge her older sister because she owed her so much. But she just couldn't work up the energy it would take to not be a drain on the family's holiday celebration.

"I'd be a drag and I'd ruin the fun and celebration for everyone. Plus, I'm boycotting Thanksgiving this year. I mean, seriously, what would I be most thankful for, my cheating man or the fact that my jerk of a boss fixed it so that I wouldn't be promoted out of his division? Finding Isaac banging another woman in my bed because he thought I was out celebrating..." Cicely let out a slow hiss of disgust.

"Oh, Cee Cee, I'm so sorry that happened to you, sweetie. You don't deserve that. If he is the kind of man who can do something like that then he doesn't deserve you, Cee Cee. I really hate to channel Gran right now, but you could be thankful that you're alive, in good health, have a family that loves you and that God saw fit to get that lying, cheating sack of trash out of your way so that you can find a good man."

Cicely sighed.

I am thankful for that. I just want a minute to myself to be in a funk. Is that too much to ask?

"I'm going to be out of the country anyway, so I can't go."

"Stop lying. Where are you going the week of Thanksgiving?"

"I'm taking an island vacation for a week to have

some me-time and to get my groove back. Sorry, I can't do the family thing this year."

"Well, think about it before you just write it off. We'll be flying out on the jet Monday morning…" Latonya's voice trailed off. "Why would you want to be on some island by yourself when you could be with your family? Are you sure traveling by yourself in your state of mind is a good idea?"

"Yep, the best idea I've had in a long time. Tell Gran I love her and I wish I could be there with you all, but I just can't."

"Okay…" Latonya seemed to be searching for another argument that would compel Cicely to say yes.

"Anyway, Peanut, now that I'm up I have *sooo* many things to take care of before my trip. So many details…" *Like actually planning a trip and booking one…. I'm going straight to hell for being a big ole liar.* "I think an island getaway is just what I need right now." *Maybe an island fling really will help me get my groove back.* "So, I'll call you when I get back. I'll have you all in my thoughts this week. You guys have a great Thanksgiving. Give my niece and nephews a big ole hug from Aunt Cee Cee and tell them I'll see them when I get back."

"But—"

"Thanks, Peanut! Love you. Bye." Cicely hung up the phone and turned it off.

She could have just stayed in the hotel and licked her wounds for the week. But the more she thought about a trip, the better it sounded. All she had to do now was make her fictional island getaway a reality.

Chapter 2

"This must be my lucky day. If it isn't Cicely Stevens," came a deep, sexy and taunting male voice from above her.

Cicely stared at the passenger waiting for her to move so that he could sit in the seat next to hers, and her heart stopped. She looked him up and down. Tall, russet brown, built like nobody's business with passionate, daring brown eyes and a mischievous dimpled smile—in a word, gorgeous.

Chase Yearwood.

It couldn't be. Fate isn't that unkind. The universe doesn't have that sick a sense of humor. If it didn't seem too totally melodramatic, she would have thrown her head to the sky and cried out, "Why?"

A weak half smile flickered across her face, and she knew it must have looked like a cross between a grimace and a sneer. Yet she couldn't force her lips to give up a full, bright but very false form of greeting to save her life. The shock of seeing *him* of all people seemed too much.

There was no way that Cicely could endure a three-and-a-half-hour flight sitting next to her arch-nemesis from college after finding out that she didn't get the promotion she'd wanted and finding her boyfriend in bed with another woman.

The timing of it all sucked. No way in hell was her biggest rival supposed to be a part of her get-away-from-it-all, soul-searching trip to Dahinda!

Granted, she probably should be on Carlton's private jet with Latonya and Gran headed for the family's Thanksgiving celebration in NYC instead of taking a solo island vacation and looking for a fling to help her get her groove back, but she couldn't bring herself to do it. She only hoped that the family would understand that she had to get away. She needed some time alone to process and reevaluate everything in her life from her failed relationships to her stymied work life. She refused to believe that she had really and truly peaked in college and there was nothing left for her to excel in.

Judging by the fact that she'd ended up sitting next to Chase Yearwood—*The Wolf,* as he'd been called in college—the universe wasn't very forgiving about her blowing off Thanksgiving with the family.

The universe is sooo freaking mean!

Chase Yearwood. Seriously? What, is Satan too busy to sit next to me on a plane to Dahinda? That was the only thing she could think of that would be worse than Chase, the devil himself.

She never thought she would see him in person again. Oh, she couldn't help seeing him in print. From the business pages to the society pages, The Wolf was media fodder. Corporate takeovers. Love them and leave them. You name it, The Wolf did it. And the press wrote about it. As far as she could tell, she was the only person in the world who could actually say that she had beaten The Wolf at his own game.

That small victory had cost her a piece of her heart.

Shouldn't have sprung for the first-class ticket, she thought as she eyed him wearily. *The Wolf wouldn't be caught dead in coach!*

Cicely got up and let Chase get into his window seat. While standing, she glanced toward the back of the plane.

Packed. Full. No chance of changing seats.

Dang.

She sat back down and fastened her seat belt,

mentally preparing herself for what could only be a very long flight.

"So, little Cicely Stevens, what have you been up to since FAMU?" The Wolf leaned back in his seat and glanced at her. A smug smirk spread across his face, showing more teeth than lip. And, oh, what perfect teeth they were.

Cicely thought about just ignoring him. Really, just because the flight was full and she couldn't move to another seat, did not mean she *had* to talk to him.

She glanced at him sideways and expelled a deep breath to let him know that she was going through great pains to speak. "After finishing my undergraduate degree I went on to get an MBA in finance. I work in finance." She crossed her arms and twisted her lips.

He squinted and opened and closed his mouth quickly. Staring at her for a second, he finally spoke. "Interesting. I would have thought that you'd be somewhere running the city by now. You know, given the way you blew into FAMU, trying to run things."

Doing a double take, she tilted her head and thought, *Trying to run things? Whatever!*

She pursed her lips a moment before responding. "Well, given the fact that I was elected student government president in the second semester of my sophomore year and I beat a guy who was going to be a senior—a fancy frat boy, sports star, and all-around Mr. Popular… Oh, wait…that was you, wasn't it? Anyway, I think it's safe to say that I didn't try, I succeeded."

He arched his eyebrow as he observed her. "Modesty has never been your strong point."

"Yours, either."

"Touché." A predatory smile, which highlighted those perfect teeth, crossed his lips. The russet-brown complexioned man with almond-shaped eyes that made a woman long for the bedroom could be likened to a taller, finer Tyson Beckford.

"So what do you say," he started and smiled at her before finishing, "we bury the proverbial hatchet and let bygones be bygones?"

Cicely pretended to consider his suggestion. There was no way she would do such a thing. Chase and his flunkies had run a horribly slanderous campaign and spread so many lies that people had still been whispering about her well into her senior year.

But the lies weren't the reason why she'd vowed never to be nice to Chase again. It was the truth that he let creep out that firmly placed him on her hate-with-a-capital-*H* list.

This time she found herself able to manage at least a fake smile. "Burying the hatchet would be the mature thing to do, huh? I mean, why hold on to silly college grudges when we're both adults."

His smile didn't appear genuine to Cicely, either. "Right. I for one am over the fact that you and your sorority sisters stole that election from me and ruined the legacy that I was going to leave for FAMU." He took a deep breath, looking all magnanimous and pompous. "I'm ready to forgive you."

Forgive me? Why, you arrogant, smug jerk! I'll show you forgive me, she thought as her right eyebrow arched slightly.

"You know, you might be on to something. I think it would be wonderful and very big of me to forgive you and your trifling fraternity brothers for running such a slanderous campaign. Especially since, even with all the lies you told, you *still* lost. Forgiving you for your lies…is…" She let out a long, exaggerated sigh before finishing, "the very least I could do. Especially since my winning the election and becoming student government association president was the beginning of the very rich legacy of dynamic leadership *I* left to FAMU."

Chase's eyes narrowed and he stared at her a full minute before his face moved and the hint of a smirk appeared.

The close quarters of the small first-class cabin seemed to move in on her with that smile.

First class was supposed to be roomy. Wasn't it? Chase and his overwhelmingly sexy, larger-than-life persona took up all the dang room. She steeled herself to his magnetism by remembering who and what he really was. An arrogant, self-serving wolf!

Cicely sighed, making strategic use of the stylized attitude that sistahs had perfected across the ages with just enough huff and a slight roll of the eyes for good measure.

"Well, I'm glad we can agree to let the past be the past. Forgive and forget," he said.

Forgive? The jury's still out. Forget? Not even on a bet.

She offered a fake laugh, a "hahahahaha" that was movie-ready. "Yes. It was a silly college rivalry, after all. Life goes on. People change."

Except for people like you. I will never forgive you for tricking me into thinking that you liked me, all the while scheming to get a picture of me kissing you to use as part of your smear campaign. "See, even opponent Cee Cee Stevens has the hots for Chase Yearwood. Cast your vote for the candidate everyone wants!"

Clearing his throat, he asked, "So, Cicely, have you been to Dahinda before?"

Cicely glanced at him. For a brief second she considered not responding.

Why are you still talking to me?

"Just briefly. I took my grandmother on a Caribbean cruise, and Dahinda was one of the islands we visited. It was so beautiful that I always wanted to come back and spend a little more time there. So, I figured I would spend a week getting to know the island."

"Well, it's my home. I was born and raised there." Chase gave her a smile that she was sure he meant to charm with. It was all teeth. "So, please allow me to be your host and tour guide, for old times' sake."

"Yeah, right." She sucked her teeth and shook her head. "I don't think so. I'd like to find my way around on my own. I'm sure you have plenty of family and friends here to keep you busy."

He leaned in close, nostrils slightly flared and eyes darkened considerably. If she didn't know any better, she would think that he was on the prowl. "Yes, but it's not often I get a chance to catch up with an old friend such as yourself. What kind of frat brother would I be if I let one of my Delta sisters roam around my island home all alone?"

She rolled her eyes then. The brother was truly reaching, trying to play the Delta and Omega connection.

"Now, you know during the years we were at FAMU the Deltas and the Omegas hardly bought into that brother-sister thing. The entire time I was there we called the Kappas our brothers. Most of my sorors couldn't stand y'all."

Nationally, the Deltas and Omegas may have had an unofficial brother and sister bond, but at

FAMU during her freshman and sophomore years and part of her junior year, the FAMU chapters of those organizations might as well have been mortal enemies. The beef between the Deltas and the Omegas was so intense the year she pledged that she wasn't required to greet members of the fraternity. In fact, she and her line sisters were expressly forbidden to greet any members of Omega Psi Phi. That year, the "Que Dogs" were on FAMU's chapter of Delta Sigma Theta's do-not-greet list. That had led to some very awkward moments for her, since she had several classes with Omegas and had to see them and not acknowledge them as fellow Greeks on the yard.

As she remembered, she realized Chase had been in one of her classes. She remembered how he would sometimes stand in her way in an effort to make her acknowledge and greet him. She would simply walk around him and not say a word.

Cicely had actually worked on building peace with the Omegas during her junior year. But Chase and his group of frat brothers had been long gone by then. The two chapters actually had a much better relationship now due to the work she had done to make peace. But she wasn't about to tell The Wolf that. It would just give him more reason to pursue what ever evil plot he had hatching in his big ole sexy head.

The smirk that came across his face let her know

he wouldn't be giving up anytime soon. "Yes. But historically our organizations have an unwritten brother-and-sister bond that I feel obligated to uphold. I just refuse to have one of my sorors wandering around Dahinda alone when I'm here to show her around."

"I'll tell you what. If I feel the need for a tour guide, I'll let you suggest the name of a good one. But I really think the time we are spending on the flight right now is enough to last us a lifetime."

Just then, the flight attendant announced that passengers could now turn on authorized electronics, and Cicely made a show of pulling out her iPod, hoping that Chase would get the hint. She figured some of the girl-power singing groups would get her though the trip and deal with Chase's annoying presence.

Cicely let out a sigh of release as she sang along with the girl groups playing on her iPod. This should make the three-and-a-half hour trip a little more bearable.

Chase watched the words coming out of Cicely's lips, but he didn't believe them for a minute. The woman wouldn't know the truth if it jumped up and bit her in the behind. He smiled at the image briefly, and then frowned when the image turned into one of him softly nipping at her shapely derriere.

She was a lying, conniving woman who had cheated

him out of his chance to be student government association president and finish his undergraduate career with a bang. She messed up his rightful place in the school's history.

There was *no way* he could possibly *still* be attracted to her.

He had always been an overachiever. He was used to obtaining everything he tried for, getting everything he wanted. He had earned his nickname, *The Wolf.* And he wore it proudly. He hadn't been born with a silver spoon in his mouth, far from it. He knew the meaning of hard work, and he played to win. Losing the election to that sweet, sexy little sophomore was a sore point in an otherwise stellar record.

Cicely Stevens owed him, he figured, as he stared at her lying lips—her soft, luscious, lying lips. It must have been his lucky day to end up sitting next to the lovely Cicely.

Cicely had pulled out an iPod and was bobbing her head to some little melody. That was fine with him. It gave him some time to study her and come up with a game plan.

"Would you like a beverage?" the curvy and jovial blonde flight attendant asked, breaking him out of his contemplation for a moment.

He tapped Cicely, who looked at the flight attendant and shook her head.

"I'll take a vodka tonic," he responded.

Vacationing in Dahinda allowed him to squeeze in a visit with family, the first since his grandmother's funeral and one of many he hoped to have in the future. Having Cicely Stevens on the same island was an unforeseen bonus.

He'd recently missed being at his grandmother's bedside with the rest of the family when she passed away. He'd had work related commitments and couldn't make it back to Dahinda in time. Leaving his job as a corporate raider, taking the job at Mainstay and his guilt about his grandmother made him consider the possibilities of changing his ways.

Chase had loved his old job. He'd loved the thrill of sniffing out companies ripe for corporate takeovers. His instincts had made for a quick rise in the business world. Although his devotion to his job had meant that he hadn't been able to make it home often. He had a spacious home that he'd built for when he visited the island, and he barely used it.

He seldom had time for a social life. But he had managed to find time for other recreational activities. He hadn't been hard-pressed to find company of the female persuasion. Fortunately, the demands of his former job meant he hadn't had the time to forge long-lasting relationships. He didn't have any intention of giving up his bachelor status any time in the near future.

Yes, women usually came and went at his command, all except for one.

He turned to Cicely, still bobbing her head and pretending to ignore him.

That she would be sitting next to him all high and mighty was a sunny side to his vacation that he hadn't expected but certainly welcomed. It was time to pay little Miss Cee Cee back for her lies and games.

This time she wouldn't get away until he was quite done with her.

She had fooled him once with her sweet idealism. He had admired her spunk in running for SGA president at the end of her sophomore year. Every time he had spoken with her, even during their heated public debates, he'd found himself liking her more and more. He hadn't intended to let her win, of course. But he could have seen her doing great things for the university in the future.

He had even considered telling his fraternity brothers to calm down on the campaign tactics, especially when she came to see him and he'd ended up kissing her. He hadn't known until later that it had been a setup.

She had paid someone to get pictures of the kiss.

Luckily, one of his fraternity brothers had been able to get a copy of the picture and their camp had used it first. It hadn't made a difference, however.

What she had come back with using the same picture of them kissing was what he felt cost him the election.

Do you really want a president who can't stop sniffing behind women long enough to properly run a campaign, let alone run the student government? Cicely "Cee Cee" Stevens will go to great lengths for FAMU, even if it means kissing a fool to get at the truth! Vote for Cee Cee and leave The Wolf to his pitiful prowl.

The truth.

That was exactly what Chase was going to devote his vacation to finding out. Cicely obviously wasn't the sweet girl he'd thought her to be. And the one kiss they'd shared had cost him the election and had haunted him for years. It was time to put all those old feelings to bed, *literally.*

He glanced at her.

She was still beautiful. Her flawless nutmeg complexion was radiant. Even that fake smile she'd given him as she lied through her teeth had an exuberance about it that pulled him in. She wore her long, dark brown hair in soft ringlet curls that framed her face. Judging by what he was able to see when she stood up so that he could get to his seat, her body had matured in all the right ways and all the right places. He didn't see the same sweet idealism in her soft brown eyes that he remembered, but they still made him want to gaze into them.

She wasn't going to make it easy, that was for sure. But then, he never liked things too easy, anyway; it spoiled the fun of the *chase*. One thing was certain, he wasn't going to miss out on the opportunity that fate had sent him to get the one who got away and pay her back for all her devious treachery.

She would crack eventually. He'd see to it.

He tapped her again and she turned to face him just as the flight attendant came back with his drink.

Cicely made a show of turning off her iPod. "What?"

Clearly that nice, sweet girl he knew back at FAMU was just an act. The way the woman was giving off attitude, you would think it was her middle name.

Chase smiled. It would take more than a *sista-girl-tude* to scare him off. "It's going to be a long flight. And even though I brought work with me, I'd much rather catch up with you. So, what brings you to Dahinda?"

"Are you serious?"

"Yes. Despite how things ended up in the past, I'd like to think that we would've been friends if we hadn't been running against one another."

She let out an exasperated sigh. "Please, you

wouldn't have even noticed me or known I was alive if I hadn't stepped up to run against you."

That certainly wasn't true. He had noticed little Miss Cicely Stevens from the first day she stepped on campus during her freshman orientation, when he'd been an orientation leader for another group of freshmen. He'd also noticed that she seemed to gravitate toward the quiet, four-eyed, nerdy-type guys. And she had run through the nerds and over them like nobody's business. He'd always thought that what she really needed was more of a challenge.

Not wanting to give her ego anything to feast on, he just let her comment about him not noticing her slide. "So, what are your plans once you land on my beautiful island?"

She paused and considered him carefully. Her eyes narrowed ever so briefly and he thought for a minute she wasn't going to answer him.

Taking her iPod and placing it in her bag, she then turned to him. "Actually, I haven't the slightest idea. This vacation was sort of spur-of-the-moment. I needed to get away from it all and needed someplace to clear my head. I figured I'd wing it."

She opened her mouth as if she were considering adding something else and then shut it quickly.

Interesting.

"Well, that just won't do, Cicely. You really have

to try and make some time for me to show you the sights. How long will you be staying?"

"One week. And while I appreciate your quite insistent offer, I really don't think I'm in the mood for any company. You know, part of the whole 'space to clear my head' thing?" She forced a fake smile and made a move to go for her iPod again.

Chase reached out and touched her hand before she could do so. An electric shock went through him, and he felt his heart skip.

Oh, shit, that was odd.

Her eyes widened and her mouth fell open, but no words came out. She shut her mouth, but she stopped reaching for her iPod. Slowly, she removed her hand from his touch.

"I'm going to be on the island for two weeks. And I'm thinking I need to spend some of that time reacquainting myself with you, Cicely. I'm not one to beg, or to force my company on a woman. But I know that you would regret it if you allowed this moment to pass without taking the chance for us to get to know one another again."

"Oh, I don't know, Chase. I'm thinking I'll live." She then quickly put the earphones back in her ears and turned on her iPod.

All Chase could do was smile at that. The trip home was already turning out to be so much more interesting than he'd thought it was going to be.

Chapter 3

For the first time ever, the girl groups weren't doing it for her. Usually, a good girl-group anthem could get her going and get her hyped enough to deal with anything the world decided to throw at her. For some reason, sitting next to Chase, she was longing for some smooth R&B love songs, some male/female duets or something equally romantic.

What the hell is that about?

There was something about sitting so close to Chase with him not being able to buy a clue and realize that she had no desire to make conversation with him that made her feel vulnerable. It made her feel like there was no way she would get off of the island of Dahinda without falling victim to The Wolf and his charms once again.

What to do? What to do? she mused as she mindlessly hummed along with the up-tempo song playing on her iPod.

She really would be crazy if she thought for a minute she should even consider her foolish— apparently not just a weak moment of her past— attraction to Chase Yearwood. He was not her type.

She turned off the iPod but didn't bother to take off the earphones or put it away.

She needed to think.

The Wolf.

Not exactly the kind of man she normally went for. In fact, she made it her business to stay far away from men like him, even before he got close enough to wound her young and impressionable heart. She hadn't been joking when she told her sister and brother-in-law that the I-love-me-some-alpha-jerk-reformed-playboys gene had skipped her. And even if it hadn't *really* skipped her, she had actively resisted the trap for years and wasn't trying to get caught up now.

But why was her allergy turning into an itch that she wanted no one but Chase Yearwood to scratch?

He wasn't a safe bet by any stretch of the imagination.

However, dating safe guys hadn't proved to be all that conflict free. They lied and cheated, too, as Isaac had shown her all too clearly.

So maybe she could take a chance and have a hot island fling with a guy *like* The Wolf. That might allow her to exorcise a whole lot of demons. She had come to the island with the vague idea of doing something wild, spontaneous, impulsive and completely unlike herself. A fling would be totally wild.

A fling with a bad boy? Even wilder...

Not a fling with The Wolf himself, of course. She knew there was no way she was ready to take him on, and she had a small feeling her heart wouldn't survive that. But someone smooth and oh-so-fine like him? That might be something she could work with.

She chanced a glance at Chase. He arched his eyebrow and then winked. She swallowed and wished she'd gotten that drink when the flight attendant had come by the first time.

Isn't first class supposed to be roomier?

Chase Yearwood just took up entirely too much room. His presence seemed just that big. She cleared her throat and tried to think about something besides how good Chase looked or how manly he smelled.

A fling, yes, but not with Chase.

"Not with Chase" needed to become her new mantra, quick, fast and in a hurry. *Not with Chase.*

Not with Chase. She chanted the words in her head like she was channeling Angela Bassett's Tina Turner at her Buddhist altar.

Chase might just be the one to lead her to her island magic man, the one to help her get past her fear of bad boys once and for all. Wolves ran in packs, didn't they? And even though she wasn't about to go there with Chase, he might have a friend that she could take on. She thought about taking him up on his offer to give her a tour of the island.

Putting the iPod away, she turned to him. "You know what, Chase? Since you've offered your help, and have been so kind about introducing me to the island, I'd love to take you up on it if the offer still stands."

"It does. I'd love to...show you the island."

The slight pause he offered before finishing his sentence made her heart still for a second.

What was that about?

Shaking it off and plastering a smile on her face, she decided to forge ahead. "Great. I'd love to hit some of the hot spots. You know, the spots where I can meet lots of people."

"Sounds good. I'd love the chance to get... reacquainted." He did that weird pause thing again and then his eyebrow arched slightly. "And I was thinking, it's the least you could do after trying to kill me."

Cicely groaned.

How did I know he was going to bring that up eventually?

"I didn't try to kill you. You were standing in front of my car and you wouldn't move."

"I was waiting for you and your line sisters to greet me." A smirk crossed his face. "You girls were pledging, and everyone knows that pledges are supposed to greet *all* Greeks on the yard. Even if you couldn't greet me as a big brother because of the strife between the sorors and the bros that year, you could have *still* greeted me."

Cicely chanced a look at him and noted the playful gleam in his eyes. Good thing he wasn't holding a grudge about her almost running him over with her car all those years ago.

Her dean of pledges had taken them to a party at a neighboring school, and Chase was there with his fraternity brothers. When she and her pledge sisters had walked by without greeting the guys, Chase had followed them out. He'd stood in front of her car, and Cicely had panicked. Sheila, the big sister whose breakup with one of the Omegas had started the feud, was in the backseat, and she told Cicely to, quote, run Chase the hell over if he didn't move. Cicely had turned to the dean of pledges, Kathy, for advice, and Kathy concurred. So Cicely had slowly inched forward in the bright red Jetta that her brother-in-law, Carlton, had purchased for her.

She remembered the wide-eyed, shocked look on Chase's face when the car started to move. And she also wouldn't forget the athletic leap he made onto the hood and the way his gleaming eyes narrowed in on her. He had jumped down from the car and she had sped off with her heart racing.

Shaking her head in hopes of shaking away the memory of his predator-like glare and all the promises of retribution his eyes held, she offered, "Like I said…er…I didn't try to kill you. You got in the way of my car."

"Yeah, right. You listened to your crazy big sisters and you almost caught a case for vehicular manslaughter." He chuckled.

Cicely decided to chance a giggle of her own since he was able to laugh about it. "Oh, I don't know. The people in my car were all ready to testify that you were crazed and must have had a death wish because you jumped in front of the vehicle like you were Superman."

They both laughed at the memory and a warm feeling came over her. Could it be that she was really feeling at ease with The Wolf? That couldn't be good. Everyone knew that as soon as the three little pigs or Little Red Riding Hood let their guards down the wolf pounced and ate them up. Still she couldn't make herself continue to hold him at arm's length.

She decided to continue their playful banter instead. "And you're lucky I didn't press charges. You dented my hood."

"Yeah, I think it was either dent your hood or end up under your wheels."

Cicely laughed. "Okay, maybe that's why I didn't press charges."

"Hmm…ya think?" His eyebrow did that sexy half slant, half arch thing again, and her mouth went dry.

"Okay. I apologize for trying to—" she cleared her throat before continuing "—kill you. That was wrong. And as penance, I guess I'll suffer your hospitality a bit on the island and let you show me around."

"Oh, you'll suffer my hospitality, will you?" He burst out into a low, sexy chuckle that sounded like a mix between a growl and a purr.

In any case, it was way too sexy for comfort.

"Yes. You're right. It's the least I can do." Cicely smiled. The fact that Chase could joke about it showed that he might not be such a bad guy after all.

"Would you like the chicken or the fish?" The flight attendant came back with the lunch entrée for the trip.

"Chicken," they answered in unison.

The flight attendant handed them both their plastic trays full of a pseudo haute-cuisine inspired chicken dish that had been microwaved to taste like plastic. She didn't even know why she bothered. She never ate airline food.

And wasn't first class supposed to have better food than this? The unappealing food was clearly another instance of the universe thumbing its nose at her.

Cutting into the rubbery chicken and overcooked veggies, she chanced another glance at Chase.

Yep, still fine.

"Now that you've apologized for trying to kill me, what do you say you add one for making me kiss you so that you could get that incriminating photo that cost me the election?" His nonchalant question had a cutting edge.

Shock caused the plastic cutlery she held to fall. Her jaw dropped. And, in a very unladylike gesture, a piece of the rubber chicken came tumbling out of her mouth and landed back in the little tray.

This was exactly why a girl should never let her guard down in the presence of a wolf!

Composing herself seemed like an unattainable goal at that moment. All she could manage was a startled, "Say what?"

Chase kept his gaze pinned on Cicely. He was finally going to get the truth about the scheming and plotting she must have done back then. He could forgive the cute little pledge who had almost run him over with a car because her big sister told her to. It had been a stupid thing for her to do, but he hadn't gotten hurt. He couldn't forgive or forget, however, the young woman who had kissed him and put those scandalous pictures in the school paper. She hadn't been pledging a sorority then. She had done those deeds on her own for her own gain.

Judging from the way her jaw was hanging, he must have caught her off guard.

Pushing his nuked airport delicacy aside, he peered at her a moment more before repeating himself. And then he waited for the apology.

The look Cicely cut him instead as she folded her arms across her chest and arched her eyebrow made him think that the apology might be a long time coming.

"If anyone should be apologizing about that photo, it's you. You are the one who orchestrated the entire thing." She let out her barrage in a heated hiss. And then a haughty indignant glare crossed her face as her shoulders crept higher and higher. "Playing on my naive emotions and catching me in a moment of weakness.... Did you and your frat brothers have a good laugh at my expense?"

"Would you like another drink, sir?" The flight attendant leaned down toward them, and he took his eyes off of the recalcitrant Cicely for a moment.

"I'll take another vodka tonic."

"And you, ma'am?"

"Gin and tonic with lime, please." Cicely smiled sweetly at the flight attendant and glared at him as soon as the woman walked off to get their drinks.

They each just stared at one another. Chase knew he was waiting for the flight attendant to return with the drinks and leave again to resume the conversation. He figured Cicely was trying to piece together her lies.

So he watched her. And she watched him.

He had to admit as he took his drink from the flight attendant and then the flight attendant handed Cicely hers, Cicely had the righteous indignation and incredulous haughty stance down. He could almost believe that she really felt that she'd been the wronged party.

Although he'd planned to use some of his time on the island to get the truth out of her, he figured he might as well get it out of her now. That way, they could get the past out and be done with it.

She was wrong and she needed to admit it.

"You're kidding, right?" Cicely asked the question between clenched teeth with her arms still firmly crossed. She hadn't even bothered to take a sip of her drink.

Chase picked up his vodka tonic, imbibing before he responded. "Do I look like I'm kidding? I mean, come on, it was a long time ago, but it would still be nice to know why you did it. Well, besides wanting to win and knowing that there was no way you would have beaten me otherwise."

She started laughing then, literally giggling out of control, holding her belly and everything.

The laughing fit went on for several minutes, and then she stopped and slowly wiped tears of laughter from her eyes. Turning, she glared at him and then put her earplugs back in and enjoyed her drink.

The nerve of him! What happened to letting bygones be bygones? Burying the hatchet? All that crap?

And then he had the nerve to try and continue his whole you-set-me-up spiel when he was the one who had set her up. He was the one who had played her and played on her feelings for him.

If it wasn't so funny it might have been sad. The man was either delusional or really thought if he put his own spin on the story long enough he could make anyone believe it, even the person who got hurt by his actions.

Oh, I'm sorry, girl. You broke your own heart. I didn't do that. And by the way, you should apologize because you hurt my little record while you were busy breaking your own heart.

The nerve!

His audacity was almost too much. Snatching off the earplugs, she turned and looked at him.

He watched her intently, his eyes studying her every move. It almost seemed like he was trying to read her, to see if she were lying.

"Why are you trying to blame me for something that you and your frat brothers cooked up? It's not my fault it backfired on you and you lost."

Loser, she thought. Even though The Wolf was anything but a loser. He might have lost that election to her, but it was probably the only thing he had ever lost in his entire life.

"Are you saying you really had nothing to do with the picture being taken?"

"How could I have known? I certainly had no idea you were going to kiss me!"

He frowned then as if he had never considered that aspect of it before. "Hmm... Maybe it was a setup," he mumbled.

"Yeah, but who could have known that we were going to kiss? I mean, we didn't plan to kiss or anything.... It was a mistake...a fluke. There's no way someone could have planned to catch us, right? Unless you knew you were going to kiss me and you planned it." Cicely didn't like the flustered jumble of her words, but she couldn't help it.

"Trust me, I didn't know I was going to kiss you that night."

Chase had a narrowly focused glint in his eyes, and he rubbed his chin in contemplation.

"After the kiss you ran off all scared, and I hung around. I didn't see anyone else there. But that doesn't mean there wasn't anyone else there. That person might have seen us kissing and taken advantage of the situation."

His thinking-man, mile-high-Private-I act had her heart stuttering. Who knew a guy putting together facts could be so sexy?

"Sounds plausible. But of course I'll have to mull it over awhile first. Given the fact that I have spent all this time pretty much despising you for using... that particular moment in your campaign, I may need a minute to rethink this new information."

"The same here. The fact that I was right about you and then led to believe that I was wrong about you, which led me to be wrong about you for all these years, is a lot to process," Chase mumbled.

"Huh?" Cicely twisted her face in a perplexed manner.

"Never mind. Let's just say I'm glad we've somewhat figured this out, because I wouldn't want anything to get in the way of us getting reacquainted."

"Right. Reacquainted." Suddenly Cicely's lips felt parched. She took a sip of her gin and tonic in an attempt to quench, if not her thirst, then something…

Chase held out his hand. "So how about the two of us form a truce for real this time?"

Cicely had to smile at that. But a small part of her wondered what would have happened if the pictures of their kiss hadn't shown up. Would they have kissed again?

"Okay. I'm sorry for hating you all these years and throwing negative energy into the universe about you."

Chase's jaw dropped. "Negative energy into the universe? Really? Now, see, I just hated you. I didn't pull a Miss Celie on you."

Now Cicely's jaw dropped. It couldn't be. One of her favorite things to do with Latonya was quote lines from black movies and plays at both opportune and inopportune moments. She crooked her pointer and middle finger and squinted her eyes. "Until you do right by me—"

"Everything you even think about gonna fail." Chase and she finished Whoopi Goldberg's famous lines in unison.

She couldn't help it. She started giggling again. "Okay, that was weird. Somebody has seen *The Color Purple* one too many times."

"And that someone would clearly be *you*," Chase said with a smirk.

"Okay, guilty as charged. I've been known to quote lines from black movies, plays, fiction and songs when I think the moment fits." Cicely giggled lightly. "It's a part of my inner dweeb. I'm like a walking Notable Quotable."

"Now I'm officially speechless. I have no idea what to do with this new information about you, Cicely. An inner dweeb?" Chase's almond-shaped brown eyes considered her and seemed to hold her. "And here I thought you were one of the cool girls? I guess that's why you used to date all those pocket-protector types in college."

Cicely's mouth fell open. "What do you mean by that?" She almost went as far as to deny her penchant for nerds, but she didn't want to let on that Chase had touched a nerve. It did bring to the forefront the question of what Chase was doing noticing the kinds of guys she dated back then.

Shaking his head as if trying to clear it, Chase smiled. "Never mind. It's not important. What is important is how you want to spend your time in Dahinda."

Yes, it's best to leave that alone. Good move, dude, good move!

"I just want to have fun. I want to do some touristy things, but I also want to see as much of the island as possible. And I'd love to see the places where the

people of Dahinda actually hang out, places off the
beaten path."

"I think I can handle that." That sexy glint
came back into his eyes, and his smile took on that
predator's gleam.

*Uh-oh. Back away from The Wolf, for your own
safety. Back away from The Wolf.*

"Honestly, Chase, you don't have to. I know you're
here visiting family. So I would totally understand if
you couldn't follow through—"

"Oh, make no mistake, I always follow through,
and there isn't anything that could keep me away
from my promise to show you around. I want to do
this very much."

The steaming sincerity in his eyes accelerated her
heartbeat until it sounded like a wild herd stampeding
in her eardrums. She couldn't think of a response
even if her mouth had been working well enough to
form words.

She cleared her throat, needing to somehow shift
the mood from this glowing nice-vibe that was
starting to develop between them. "So, I've been
hearing lots of buzz about you through the years,
lots of corporate takeovers, forced mergers, raiding
and moneymaking. Very impressive, Yearwood."

There, she'd said it!

The last thing she wanted to do was give Mr. Very
Big Ego another reason to have a swelled head. But

his career was impressive, and she envied it like nobody's business. That's why losing the promotion stung so much. She wanted to play with the big boys like Chase, and had essentially been told, *no, stay in your lane, little girl.*

Chase squinted and eyed her for a moment before responding. "Thanks. I had no idea that you'd kept up with my career."

Big. Ego. Indeed. "I wasn't keeping up with your career or anything like that. I just noticed a couple of articles every now and then and thought I'd make small talk since we're on the plane for three hours. No need to go getting the big head, Chase."

He gave her one of his trademark sexy grins then, and she felt her insides quiver.

"Oh, in that case, thanks. What about you? You're in finance, right? What do you do? Are you moving and shaking like you did in undergrad?"

She swallowed. It was like every school reunion nightmare she'd ever had rolled into one. She was the loser who had peaked in college, forced to face Mr. Most Successful.

No. Way.

"Yes, I work in finance, but I'm on vacation now. The last thing I want to talk about is work. So, if you're going to hang with me at all this week, that's the first rule. No talking about work while we're on vacation."

"Sounds fine with me. No talking about work."
He held out his hand and she shook it.

An oh-so-pleasing electric charge coursed from
her hand through her body again, and she felt her
eyes flutter.

She looked him in the eye and she could tell that he
felt the electric charge, too. His eyes were narrowed
and his jaw was tight, as if he was trying to fight the
feeling. She sighed in relief. As long as they both
decided to resist whatever the attraction was between
them, then things should be okay.

God forbid either one of them would decide to let
go and give in to the heat.

Chapter 4

Okay, now how exactly did I wind up letting Chase talk me into taking a ride to my hotel in his rental instead of taking a cab?

The convertible sports car let the island breeze in to tousle her hair. On a regular day, a sister would have been a tad bit upset about messing up *the do*. But there was something about the company and general feel of the moment that made Cicely think it was okay to sacrifice the roller set she'd gotten a couple of days ago.

Glancing around, she noted that the pastures and cows along the road from the airport made for a different landscape from the port in Sansport she remembered from when she'd visited the island on her cruise. Once they pulled onto the highway, it at least appeared that they were moving away from the rural countryside.

"So, what are your plans for dinner tonight?" Chase kept his eyes on the narrow road, but his voice held a strong hint of interest.

"I haven't made any plans for dinner. I'm just winging it. I sort of took this trip on the spur of the moment." *Way to sound flighty, Cee Cee.* "I mean, I wanted to experience spontaneity, you know. Do something out of my ordinary."

"That sounds risky. Are you sure you're up for it?"

"Oh, I'm sure. I've already got some plans to make this the most exciting excursion of my life."

Why are you telling him this, girl?

"Really?" Chase laughed. "I can't even imagine that. Plus, if you have 'plans,' doesn't that sort of go against the whole spontaneous aspect? And you really don't strike me as the cast-cares-to-the-wind, let-go-and-let-flow type. You're one of those by-the-book sisters. I bet you try to *plan* everything. And you probably have a bunch of rules that you follow religiously and try to make others follow them, as well."

Taken aback for a moment, she wondered, *How does he know?*

Watching him drive, with his chin tilted all smugly, caused her indignation to sprout. She could throw caution to the wind just as much as the next girl! And who was Chase, anyway, to think he had her all figured out, put in a box and tied with a neat bow? She could be just as wild as anyone else.

Really she could.

Cicely decided it was time to let Mr. Know-It-All in on her real plans for her island stay. She would need his help locating the hot spots, anyway. And he had offered to show her around.

"I'm thinking I'll have an island fling while I'm in Dahinda. And I would love it if you could take me somewhere where I can meet someone to fit the bill." Once the words fell out of her mouth, she thought about calling them back.

Chase's head turned sharply, and he gawked at her.

"Eyes on the road, dude!"

"Okay." Shaking his head as if he was trying to clear it, Chase let out an uneasy chuckle. "You just shocked me for a minute."

Cicely tilted her head.

That's right, baby boy! I can be spontaneous.

"I don't know what's so shocking about it. Women of the world have affairs all the time. It's the new thing. Don't you watch television? Step into the twenty-first century, dude."

She could see his face twisting up in weird contortions even from his profile. Each frown, open and close of his mouth and purse of his lips made her squirm just a little bit more in her seat.

Cicely started to rethink her plan. Why was she asking Chase Yearwood, of all people, to help her find someone to have her get-your-groove-back fling with? Wasn't that a bit like the three little pigs asking the big bad wolf to help them rebuild their homes? Maybe it wasn't such a bright idea after all.

She knew she had made a colossal mistake when Chase pulled the car off the highway at the next exit. After finding a nice, quiet, rural spot, he stopped.

He parked the car, took several breaths and looked at her with his eyebrows arched ever so slightly.

"Let me get this straight. You want me—" he paused and pointed to himself for emphasis "—to help you—" he squinted and waved his hand in her direction "—find a man to have a hot island fling with?"

"Well, yeah. You're the one who said you wanted to look out for a soror. Yada, yada, yada. Help a sister get to know your island.… Let bygones be bygones. Blah, blah, blah."

If she had a collar on her shirt it probably would have been tight right about then. Instead she just felt a slow heat rising from her neck to her face. If she'd been a little lighter in complexion, she would have been turning ten shades of red. Leave it to Chase to make her feel uneasy and on edge.

Chase couldn't help staring at Cicely. He hadn't expected such a request to come from her mouth. He'd actually thought he would have to be creative and find ways to get close to her.

She'd unwittingly provided him with the perfect in. He wasn't a big believer in fate. But meeting up with Cicely on the plane and having her share her outrageous plan for him to help her find someone to have an island affair with would certainly make a believer out of him. Because the only person little Miss Cicely was going to be having a fling with in Dahinda was him.

Touching his hand to his chin, he studied her. She seemed a little flustered. He figured she was having second thoughts, and he couldn't allow that. "So, what exactly are you looking for in an island fling?"

"Huh?"

Her mouth fell open, and he couldn't help noticing the sexy fullness of her lips. To kiss them again would be divine. He couldn't wait.

"You know. What type of man are you looking for? I think I remember something about your tastes back in college." Boy, did he remember. He wished he could forget. "You like those pocket-protector type of brothers don't you?"

"I...do...not! I mean...normally...I do...but... well..." Uncomfortable didn't even begin to describe the flustered look in her eyes and the quick opening and closing of her luscious mouth.

She closed her eyes and took a deep breath, and then she turned and stared him right in the eye. "That's my usual preference. I have more in common with men who don't live by the notches on their bedposts. But for my fling, I'm thinking I'll take a walk on the wild side. If only for the week I'm here..."

"Are you sure you can hang? No offense, but you don't look like the wild-side type. Definitely not the fling type."

No, little Cicely, you are the until-death-do-us-part type. A guy would have to be silly or ready to play Russian roulette with his bachelorhood to get into a fling with you. But pass me the gun and label me stupid, because I'm all in.

Chase tapped the steering wheel as he waited for her response.

She sighed in contemplation. "That's the thing. Usually, I'm not. But let's just say I've had an awakening of sorts. And I learned that life doesn't last forever. I also learned that sometimes we should dive ahead into uncharted territory in order to make it possible to really move on."

*Psychobabble. Somebody's been watching a little
too much Oprah.*

He'd never thought he'd have a reason to thank
daytime television. But then, he'd never thought he'd
have Cicely Stevens boxed, gift wrapped and handed
to him with a bow.

Thank you, Oprah, Dr. Phil, whoever!

"Okay. So, what are you looking for?" Trying to
hold back the wide grin that threatened to surface
proved to be hard work.

"Well…I guess I'm looking for a bad boy. Someone
like…well…you…ah…you know, someone who can
take me places I have yet to even imagine." A small
bead of sweat appeared on her brow as she turned
away from him. She swallowed several times and
then turned back to face him. "I just want to have an
experience for once in my life that is totally outside
of the norm, totally unlike anything that I would *ever*
do."

Chase studied the woman sitting next to him,
looking for the catch. She had to be playing with
him, right? No way was fate that much in his favor.
He took a whiff of the sweet island air and smiled. He
should have made it back home a lot more often.

"Are you serious about this?"

She paused for a moment, fiddling with her seat
belt. After a deep breath she stated, "I have never
been more serious about anything in my life."

"Okay, Cicely. You have got yourself a deal. I promise you, I won't rest until you have experienced an island fling that will blow your mind and take you to another world."

She didn't need to know at that moment that he'd decided that he was going to be the one to take her there and deliver the fling. All she needed to know right then was that she had a helper.

"Great, then…ah…I mean…I know you're visiting your family and all, and I don't want to intrude on their time." She tried crossing her sexy legs, but the space in the small sports car didn't allow for much movement. It did allow him to get a good glimpse of her long, shapely limbs and to imagine all the ways they could wrap around him.

She licked her lips in a nervous gesture, and he felt a tightening in his gut.

"So if you can't escort me to the spots, just point me in the right direction. Once I find my fling-man, then I won't need to bother you anymore."

"Oh, I'm sure I can spend time with the family and help you find what you're looking for, as well." Intrigued, Chase leaned over. "In fact, I think finding the proper man for you to have this little tryst with is going to be super easy. I think I might have someone in mind."

"Really? Well…that's…wonderful."

"I know. I think he's just what you're looking for. Just what you need."

"Just so long as we're clear that I'm looking for a no-promises, no-commitment-required, no-questions-asked fling. I just want to let my hair down and have fun for once in my life. You know?"

"Yes, I know. And like I said, I'd even be willing to escort you to the island hot spots and clubs."

"Cool. I can't wait."

"Neither can I. Neither can I."

The vacation had taken on a very interesting slant and a promising turn indeed. Chase pulled back onto the road with a big smile on his face.

Chapter 5

Cicely stood out on the balcony of her hotel room and inhaled. The sweet island air was intoxicating. From her balcony she could see the white sand beach and miles and miles of the brightest, most serene turquoise waters she'd ever seen.

When she'd visited Dahinda a few years back as a port of call on a cruise, she had only had a few hours to explore the island. She and her grandmother had taken a bus excursion that gave them a tour of just about the entire small island, from the lush inner island to the miles and miles of beaches.

The people were so friendly and the food, much like the food on the other Caribbean islands she had traveled to, was absolutely to die for. She'd known then that she would one day come back and stay for a longer period of time. She just didn't know that one of Dahinda's native sons, her archrival, would insinuate his way into her trip.

She exhaled and inhaled again. *Chase Yearwood.*

She smiled almost ruefully and wrapped her arms around herself. She still remembered the first argument she'd ever had with him, when she was a sophomore in college and full of wide-eyed idealism. She wasn't normally prone to outbursts or arguments, so her intense reactions to Chase always kept her just a little bit off-kilter.

Hearing the knock on her door, she left the balcony to go and answer it. She couldn't contain the grin that crossed her face when she saw Chase there.

He'd said he'd give her a driving tour of the inner island and take her to his mother's rum shack that evening. She doubted that she would find her potential fling partner in the rum shack, but she didn't want to be rude. And she also didn't want to rule out the chance that her fling could be waiting to be found in Chase's mother's rum shack.

She'd put on a light and airy maxi-style sundress in bold shades of red, orange and yellow with some red, medium-heeled strappy sandals. She'd pulled her hair up in a quick French twist with some lose tendrils around her face to relax the look. She was glad she'd taken the time to shower and dress up a little when she got a look at Chase.

He wore a short-sleeved, cream silk shirt and perfectly pressed cream linen shorts with a very expensive pair of brown leather sandals. The cream of his clothing and the warm, earthy russet-brown tone of his skin combined to make one amazing package. The short sleeves of his shirt and the length of his shorts revealed just enough of his very muscular arms and legs. The bit of skin that she could see hinted at more and more muscles and more and more delectable brown skin.

She blinked as she tried to rid her mind of the image of those toned, muscular and very fit arms and legs wrapped up with her own arms and legs.

What would that feel like?

She shook her head as she smiled.

She would never know.

"Hi" was the only word she could come up with.

"Hi." He stared at her and for a minute she felt like time had ceased to move. His almond-shaped eyes seemed to caress her. She could feel his eyes' movement on her skin as they roamed her body. She felt her pulse quicken as she noted the subtle rise and fall of his massive chest.

"Are you ready to ride around some of the island?"

"Yes, let me grab my purse and we'll be good to go. I can't thank you enough for this, Chase. I know I'm not your favorite person. So it means a lot to me that you are willing to give me a tour and help me find my way around the island."

"Like I told you before, it's definitely my pleasure. We have a lot to catch up on." His smile seemed genuine, and it put her mind at ease.

She followed him to his convertible, and he held the door open for her. Once they started rolling they let the silence speak. She didn't trust what she might say, and she had no idea what he was thinking. The way he had looked at her a few minutes ago made her feel hotter than she had ever felt for any man, ever.

That was a big problem.

Massive.

No matter what kind of attraction they were feeling, there was still the fact that they didn't like one another. They may have called a tentative truce, but in reality she still didn't believe that he trusted her.

And she knew she would be a fool to trust him.

"If you look over to your right you'll see one of the old sugar cane plantations. The government turned the mansion into a museum. And the land no longer produces crops for mass harvesting and sugar production. But tourists can come here and get the experience of chopping a piece of sugar cane, tour the old mills and refineries."

Cicely smiled because she and Gran had toured the plantation as a part of their cruise excursion, and she had actually held a machete and chopped a piece of sugar cane.

"I did the tour during my short visit. It was very informative. And the pictures and artifacts of the slaves and indigenous people…wow! What they must have gone through back then. It really breaks your heart." Cicely shivered at the memory. Thinking about the way the colonists had systematically murdered native island people and enslaved African people to work on the island always made her sick inside.

"Yes, there is a lot of rich and painful history on this small island." Chase seemed a bit shaken by the cruelty of the history, as well. "Now, this area here is pretty much a small residential area. My mom and aunts have homes here. I had them built for them."

The homes were gorgeous. Some were built of white stones while others were coral pink and peach stones. They were one- and two-story homes with intricate island designs and were clearly meant to withstand hurricane seasons and look good while doing so.

"Did you grow up in this area of the island?"

"No. We lived in a much poorer section where mom still has her rum shack. No matter how much money I make and send her, that woman still won't give up her business." Chase chuckled. "At least she took the house here and let me remodel her business. I wanted to build her a house near mine on the beach, but she wouldn't hear of it."

"She sounds like my grandmother. My sister and her husband have been trying to get her to let them build her another house in Miami, but she refuses to leave her little house in Overtown. She's like, 'I worked my fingers to the bone to pay for it, and it's mine.'"

"Sounds like my mother. I had to build the house and have her sisters furnish it the way my mom would like before she agreed to move into it."

"That sounds like my gran. I purchased a cruise for her a few years back—that's when I first visited Dahinda. Anyway, before that, she would never get on a plane and she darn sure wasn't getting on a boat and sailing across the ocean. She was of the, 'God put me on land and made me from the earth. I'm gonna stay on the ground until the good Lord sees fit to have me returned to the earth' school of thought. She wasn't trying to be in the air or in the sea." Cicely laughed remembering her grandmother's colorful arguments about why the only thing she was getting in was a car and how she didn't totally trust those, either.

"But I went and purchased a cruise for the two

of us anyway, and my sister and I both talked her into going. Since she didn't want to see me waste my hard-earned pennies, she went. The only thing she couldn't stand worse than the thought of getting on a boat or plane was wasting hard-earned money. Now girlfriend takes at least one cruise a year, maybe even two. And my sister has Gran flying now. She's a regular jet-setter!"

Chase chuckled at Cicely's depiction of her grandmother. She sounded a lot like his own grandmother. That woman had never stepped off of Dahinda because she had refused to get on a plane or boat. Once again he felt the pang of guilt that came whenever he thought about her and the fact that he hadn't been able to be at her bedside when she died because he'd had a big merger to oversee at work.

"Sounds like we both come from humble beginnings and have managed to do better for our-selves and our families." He wasn't sure how he felt about that.

The less he found himself identifying with the very tempting Cicely Stevens the better. She was probably the same as all the other scandalous women he had dealt with in the past, maybe even worse. She had actually beaten him before, and she might have done so by nefarious means. He still wasn't sure he bought the theory they'd come up with on the plane.

Without proof of who took the picture and why,

Cicely and he had an uneasy truce, at best. He needed to keep that firmly in mind.

Chase parked the car beside his two-story home, located on a private beach.

They had driven around the island chatting and had pretty much forgotten about the tour part of it. They were just riding, talking and letting the island breeze entice them with the possibilities that lay ahead.

"This is my home. I usually stay here when I visit. I don't get to make it back often, but it's still nice to have a place that's all mine on the island." He turned to her and smiled. "Would you like a quick tour of my home before we go to my mom's spot?"

He could see that she seemed to be at war with herself as she tried to decide how she was going to answer his question.

He smiled as he watched her put one foot in front of the other, slowly.

Did she dare walk willingly into the wolf's lair?

Things were not going exactly as Chase had planned. He had offered to show Cicely around his small island in hopes that spending time with her would either get him to come to his senses and not want to pursue her *or* get her to see that the man she needed to be having an affair with was him. His mind fluctuated between the two, and he was determined to find some type of closure or solace in one or the other.

Her dress, however, wasn't helping him keep a clear head.

He never would have thought that something so long and flowing could look so damn sexy. But it was kind of low-cut. And it did show her beautiful, long, elegant arms. And her hands…her hands with that neat and proper French manicure that gave no hint at all that when your eyes traveled to her pretty little feet you'd find blazing red nails on the toes sticking out of those sexy sandals.

Man, he had it bad.

He just hoped it didn't come back to bite him in the behind. And now he was inviting her into his sanctuary, a place sacred to him even though he barely ever came here, a place where the only other women who had ever set foot in had been relatives. He had a feeling the place would never be the same again once Cicely stepped inside. But damned if he could stop his hand from reaching out for hers and leading her inside.

He let her walk slightly ahead of him and watched the gentle sway of her hips as she made her way through the entryway. He shook his head and again wondered if he was doing the right thing. Maybe he should just call things off and let her fend for herself this week. No need to tempt fate and give

Cicely Stevens the chance to get the better of him yet again.

He cleared his throat. "I don't get to spend a lot of time here at all. In fact, it's been several months since my last trip home, for my grandmother's funeral. The job kept me really busy. But I always knew I had this place to come to whenever I needed a break."

"I'm sorry to hear about the loss of your grandmother, Chase." Cicely reached out and stroked his arm.

She smiled at him as she looked around his home. "This place is absolutely amazing. How do you manage to stay away? If I had a place like this overlooking that beautiful beach, I'd be here every single day." Cicely walked around, taking in the sparsely decorated room.

He'd gone for a minimalist design because the real beauty came from outside of the home. There were several open, airy areas and lots of windows. The furniture was all white with bold splashes of earth tones—from clay to deep mahogany—acting as accents. A white sectional sofa flanked the living room, and the walls were all off-white with a few select Caribbean-inspired paintings gracing them.

They walked through his home in silence. She marveled at various points along the way. Her eyes were appreciative, and her smile seemed to make the already bright and airy home even brighter. As he surveyed his home through her eyes, he couldn't help pondering her earlier question and wondering why he didn't make a point of coming home more often.

When they reached his bedroom she touched the king-size mahogany four-poster bed and grinned.

"Okay, that has to be the most comfortable-looking bed I've ever seen. How do you manage to keep all this white clean? You must be some kind of neat freak or something."

He grinned back at her feeling more at ease than he should have. It was on the tip of his tongue to invite her to try out the bed and see how comfortable it really was. He imagined her spread out on the plush white comforter. He knew if he actually saw her in his bed, they wouldn't make it to his mother's rum shack. So he tried his best to get the image out of his head.

"Actually, I'm not really that neat. I'm hardly here, and when I am here, the white furnishings make me extra careful."

She giggled. "That bed is so plush it makes you want to just dive into it, like a cloud or something."

He could see diving in all right, and it wasn't her into his bed but rather him into her.

He shook his head. "So, we should probably head on out to my mom's place. I should warn you, it's not very fancy. But the people are really nice and the food is the best you'll probably get on the entire island. There's a small dance floor, and some nights she even has karaoke."

"Sounds like fun, especially the food part. I'm ready for some Caribbean fare." She rubbed her virtually nonexistent belly.

For some reason he held out his hand for her again, and when she took it he felt that electric charge again. As they walked out of his home hand in hand, he knew it was going to be a long week.

As soon as they walked into Chase's mother's rum shack, Cicely relaxed. It was jam-packed with people, and everyone was just casually having fun. Some people were at the bar having drinks; others were at tables eating, talking and playing cards. Some people were even on the very small dance floor swaying to the reggae music that wafted from the back corner of the dance floor where a deejay was playing.

Judging from the fresh paint outside, the beautiful sign that read Margie's Rum Shack and the artfully decorated interior, Chase's mom must have let him spend a good bit of money on decorating and upkeep. The place was small but stylish. It wasn't the typical dive.

The color scheme and decor were warm and welcoming, with soothing greens and blues making up the bulk of the walls. The space was accented in bold oranges and reds. The tables, chairs and barstools were all a deep cherrywood. The floor was a bleached-blond plank that made the other colors pop. Pictures of various reggae and calypso singers graced the walls. Some of them were signed, and a woman who must have been Chase's mom was in some of them with the famous singers.

"Well, look what the cat drug in. I haven't seen this one since Jesus was a baby. How are you, Chase?" An older gentleman with a shock of gray hair stood up as they entered and walked over. He shook Chase's hand and they embraced.

"Mr. Frank, it's good to see you, as always. I'm fine. It's good to be home. This is my friend Cicely." Chase moved aside so that Cicely could shake Mr. Frank's hand.

"Hold the phone! My son brought a woman home? Get out! Well, I don't believe it!" A tall, plump woman in a beautiful tropical-colored silk short set came running from behind the counter carrying a white terry cloth towel with her. "San, watch the bar while I go and check this out for myself, because I don't believe it."

"Margie, you're gonna embarrass the boy. No wonder he never brings any girls home for you to see." Mr. Frank shook his head as he made his way back to his seat at the bar.

"Man…know my place and mind your business! This is my son. If I want to embarrass him from here to the countryside of Dahinda, I can do it. I'm the one who went through a whole day of labor to bring him into this world." Chase's mother rolled her eyes at Mr. Frank before turning her attention back to Chase and Cicely.

Chase pulled his mother into his arms. "Don't start, Ma. You know Mr. Frank is the only one who can put up with your mood swings. If he gets tired of you, what other man will have you?"

Margie squeezed Chase in her arms before popping him upside the head with her cloth. "How can you come here with your girlfriend and not give me any warning? You know I have to fix myself up to meet my future daughter-in-law—"

"Ohhhhh, nooooo!" Cicely found the correction falling out of her mouth before his mother could even finish what she was saying. "We are just friends.... I mean, we're not dating or anything like that." She was shaking her head so profusely she hoped her French twist didn't fall out.

Margie gave her a once-over. "She's pretty, though. Sweet enough, but not too sweet on you, it seems, my handsome son. Not too bright though…if she doesn't see what a catch you are!" Margie chuckled and shrugged. "I like her, though. If only she knew she's the first woman you ever brought here, so that must mean you have designs on her that she doesn't know about."

Margie laughed a deep belly laugh that would

have been contagious and made Cicely join her if she didn't have a gut feeling the laugh was on her.

Chase had turned to look at Cicely when she blurted out her very loud "ohhhhh, nooooo," and Mr. Frank was watching her closely, too. In fact, it seemed like all the eyes in the small rum shack were now firmly planted on Cicely.

"Cicely's just a friend, Ma." Chase's voice was picking up more of the island cadence as he interacted with his mom. "I went to school with her and met up with her on the plane. She's a Yankee, and I felt it was only hospitable for me to show her around our beautiful island. Everyone, this is Cicely Stevens from Miami. Cicely, this is everybody."

Margie eyed her son suspiciously. "Mmm-hmm. If you say so."

She took Cicely's arm. "So, Cicely Stevens from Miami, come to the bar and let me chat you up a bit. I need to learn everything I can about you just in case…"

"Ma…" Chase warned.

Margie sucked her teeth in a long, lyric way. "What? I just want to get to know the girl like I know all my customers here in Margie's Rum Shack. Man, leave me alone, hear? Know my place before I kick you out of it."

Chase laughed at that as he followed Margie and

Cicely to the bar. "You wouldn't kick your only beloved son out of here."

Margie laughed. "In a heartbeat, you rascal!" She reached out her other arm and pulled Chase along with her. She sat them side by side at the bar and started walking toward the back room. "I'm going to fix you each a plate, and then I'm coming back to learn all about Miss Cicely from Miami."

Mr. Frank moved from his previous seat and came and sat on the other side of Cicely. The older man took a sip of his drink and then asked, "So, how long you staying, Chase?"

"I'll be home for two weeks. Long enough for you all to get good and tired of me." Chase chuckled.

Mr. Frank nodded. "That's good. It's good to have you back."

Chase nodded, too. "Good to be back."

Margie came out with two plates of steaming hot food that smelled heavenly. Cicely tried to strategize a way that she could tear into her food and still maintain some kind of cuteness, but there was just no way. The scents of curry, cumin and spicy peppers assaulted her nose, and her mouth had to strike back.

She dug in. But at least she also got around to telling Margie that the food was delicious and thanking her for it before she was too far gone.

"Nothing like a woman who can appreciate a good meal," Mr. Frank offered with a wide grin.

"Yes, I like Cicely from Miami." Margie seemed to be studying her with appreciation. "So, Cicely, you knew my son from his college days, huh?"

Cicely swallowed and wiped her hands on her napkin even though she wanted to lick the juices of the delectable food off of her fingers.

"Yes, he was a little ahead of me. But we were both at FAMU around the same time. We had a little rivalry going, though. So we weren't exactly the best of friends." She took another bite of her food while she could.

"What? A woman on this earth who didn't like my Chase?" Margie let loose one of her big belly laughs again. "Now, that's a first. This boy has had women and girls running after him ever since he was twelve, maybe even eleven." Margie went behind the bar and fixed Chase a drink. "What are you drinking, Cicely?"

"I'll take a Dandy. In the bottle is fine." Cicely noticed that both Margie and Chase's eyes lit up when she asked for the island's locally brewed beer.

"Well, look at her. Chase, I thought you said she was a Yankee and didn't know anything about Dahinda! Look at how she's coming in here just as smooth as you please, asking for our beer!" Margie chuckled as she pulled out a nice frosty bottle of Dandy, opened it and placed it in front of Cicely.

"Girl, what you know about a Dandy?" Chase

laughed. "Dandy may sound like a light and fun drink, but it's not like those weak Yankee beers. You better watch yourself. We make them strong here."

Cicely let her eye wander to his bulky and very muscular forearms and thought, *you ain't never lied....*

"So, Cicely, tell us a little more about how you know Chase. You met in school and you didn't care for him too tough, huh? What happened next, he wore you down and you dated for a while before breaking up, and then you saw each other on the plane and realized that you wasted too much time apart—"

Laughing, Chase shook his head. "Ma, you need to lay off the soap operas. It's not even that deep. She's just a friend."

"Exactly! Really-really new friends at that..." Cicely felt the need to clarify further. "I mean... well...we're just starting to build a friendship after years of not liking one another. I don't even know why he's being nice to me. I almost think he's setting up some kind of trap. That's what he did when we were in college and I ran against him for student government president."

Margie's eyes went wide, and she pointed at Cicely with her mouth open. "Hey, hey, wa-it! Are you the one who beat my Chase in the election for student government president in college?" Margie seemed to be momentarily awed. "Well, I never thought I would meet you. Girl, you had my son so distraught, hear. He'd never lost anything at all until he lost that election to you."

Cicely took a swallow of her beer and gulped.

Uh-oh was all she could think as she felt Chase stiffen beside her.

She hadn't known it had been *that* deep for Chase. She almost felt a little guilty that she had beaten him. *Almost.*

"Personally, I think it was good for him to finally lose something. He needed to see that he didn't have to win all the time," Margie opined.

"I don't believe this! My own mother…" Chase's eyes were wide with feigned shock. "This is a sad day, people of Dahinda, a sad day, indeed."

Cicely laughed. "Clearly, the universe had to send a little message to Mr. Overachiever and used me to do it."

Chase glared at Cicely when his mother let out another belly-busting laugh.

"Hey, don't shoot the messenger." Cicely placed her hands up in mock innocence before going back to her plate of food.

After she polished off the plate of rice and peas, fried flying fish and fried plantains, she couldn't help rubbing her stomach in satisfaction. "Ms. Yearwood, this food was amazing. You're going to have me coming back here every night for dinner! This is probably the best Caribbean food I've ever had, and I live in Miami, so that's saying a lot."

"Thank you, Cicely. You can come back anytime you want. You're always welcome here. And call me Margie, girl. We don't stand on ceremony here at Margie's Rum Shack. Now tell me, what can we do to make you like my knuckleheaded son? He's real hardheaded and can work your nerves more than a little bit. But I think you're just the one that can finally tame the *so-called* Wolf." Margie let out another laugh and reached over to touch Chase's face lovingly.

Chase allowed his mother to stroke his cheek, and Cicely thought it was the most endearing thing she'd ever seen. She smiled at the two of them. Mother and son, it was too cute!

When Chase looked at Cicely, his eyes narrowed ever so slightly. If she wasn't so attuned to him, she might have missed it. His expression was a mixture of the desire she'd seen a while back, a hint of irritation and something else she couldn't name.

"Well, Ma, if Cicely thinks she's up for the task, I'm more than willing to see if she can *really* tame me." Chase offered his sexy, cocky little smile-sneer thing along with that look of his.

This time she could clearly name the something else she saw in his gaze…

Challenge!

The only question was…was she really up for taking on his challenge?

Chapter 6

Chase watched Cicely on the small dance floor with his mother, Mr. Frank and a few other customers. She was teaching them how to do the cupid shuffle, of all things!

He couldn't remember the last time he'd seen his mother dance. She looked happy, and he supposed he should be happy about that. And he would have been if Cicely didn't have the entire rum shack, filled with all his friends and family members, eating out of the palms of her hands, her sexy, sexy little hands.

Watching them all doing the cupid shuffle was just that margin over too-damn-much.... He had watched the line dance craze take off when the reggae version

of "Electric Boogie" came on, and he tolerated it
when his mother pulled Cicely onto the dance floor
and they all did the electric slide. He grinned and
bore it when Cicely got the deejay to put on the O'Jays
song "Living for the Weekend" and taught them all
another line dance. But when she had the deejay find
"Cupid Shuffle" and taught them the dance…well…
that had been the last straw.

His mom and everyone else seemed to love Cicely,
and Cicely seemed to be having the time of her life.
Chase was irritated and frustrated, and he couldn't
figure out Cicely or how he felt about her. He was
still vacillating between putting the past behind them
and pursuing her or keeping his hard-won and well-
nourished resentment firmly in mind and not trusting
her as far as he could see her.

The only problem was, what he could see of her
bouncing happily around the dance floor looked
too damn sexy and made him want her too damn
much.

He took a sip of his drink just as the "Cupid
Shuffle" went off and saw Cicely laughingly make
her way over to the deejay again. He rushed over
before she could tell the man to play whatever she
was going to tell him to play.

"How about a slow jam, Donnie?" Chase asked
the deejay.

He pulled Cicely into his arms before she could

complain and held her close as the deejay put on a slower song.

His mother rolled her eyes at him and was making her way back to the bar when Mr. Frank pulled her into his arms.

Margie and Mr. Frank whispered to one another and laughed as they danced and watched Chase and Cicely. Chase really hoped that one day his mother would give in and break away from whatever it was that was making her too scared to accept Mr. Frank's many proposals of marriage.

Mr. Frank had been around ever since Chase had been a preteen, and he hadn't gone anywhere yet. The man was the closest thing Chase had to a father figure.

"Hey, I was about to teach them the cha cha slide," Cicely complained, but she didn't pull away from him. If anything, she melded closer into his arms.

"You can teach them another time. Don't think my mother will let you leave this island without coming back to see her. My family really seems to like you, Cicely."

"Well, I hate to be conceited, but most people do tend to like me, Chase. I'm highly likable. If a person doesn't like me, then that person, nine times out of ten, has issues."

He narrowed his eyes at that until he saw the

telltale smirk on her face that said she was probably joking. He laughed and pulled her closer.

"So, what's this nonsense with you going out of your way to downplay our friendship to my folks?"

"What? We barely like each other. We're bitter rivals and probably will remain bitter rivals until the end of time. The only thing keeping us from a fight to the death is that the stakes of a student government president campaign from years ago just aren't that high. But I know you didn't really mean it when you said we had a truce."

"Yeah? And how do you know that?"

Her smile radiated sunshine and warmed him from the inside out. "Because I didn't mean it. I still blame you for that picture and for using that kiss and obvious slip of my standards to ruin me." She tried to pull away, clearly trying to escape.

But there was no way he was going to let her get away with that little whopper. He pulled her closer and stared down at her. "So basically we are back were we started? You really believe that I orchestrated the whole thing. I planned to kiss you and had someone waiting to take a picture? And then I planned to use it to somehow try and beat you in the campaign?"

"Yes. After all, you kissed me. I didn't kiss you."

This was getting interesting.

He stared at her, licking his lips at the memory.

"Oh, you kissed me back, little Cicely. I damn sure remember you kissing me back. Let's talk about this outside where there aren't so many ears around."

Cicely felt the cool island breeze coming over her, and she could hardly maintain her indignation at Chase. He was sooo irritating. Why'd he have to make her dance with him and all that?

She had been doing a great job of pretty much, for the most part, forgetting he even existed. *Well, almost.* How could she really forget with him standing at the bar, watching her with that look of challenge in his eyes? That smooth, sexy predator thing he had going was pretty hard to forget. And now he had her standing outside of the rum shack, away from all her newfound friends and allies.

"I don't know why you want us to rehash this again and again if you're not going to admit to what you did." She crossed her arms and glared at him.

He sneered. "Because, now that I think about it, I remember more about that night. If your silly soror Sheila hadn't gotten a guilty conscience and called Jonathan, we wouldn't have even gotten the picture in the first place!" He gave her a pointed stare. "She gave us the pictures because, and I quote, 'I felt what the sorors were doing was wrong and I wanted to try and make amends.'"

"Yeah, right. Sheila was the one who gave us the pictures and let us know what you all were planning.

She said she had a momentary slip and fell for Jonathan's apologies and found the pictures in his dorm room after she heard you guys hatching your plan."

Suddenly back in that moment, Cicely realized that Sheila was the only one who knew about the meeting with Chase. Sheila had been acting as Cicely's campaign manager and had set up the meeting.

"Sheila." Cicely muttered the name at the same time as Chase did, and they found themselves staring at one another again.

"Sheila set it up," Chase mumbled.

"Yeah, but she couldn't have known that we were going to kiss. I mean, we didn't… It was a mistake, a fluke… There's no way she could have planned that." That was the part that still troubled her.

"You're right. She couldn't have. But she was supposed to meet us there along with my campaign manager. We were all supposed to be going over the debate." Chase's eyes narrowed, and he rubbed his chin in contemplation.

"After the kiss you ran off, and I hung around to let Steve and Sheila know that we would have to reschedule. Sheila never showed. But Steve did eventually. I'm thinking Sheila showed up when we were kissing and took the pictures then."

"Sounds plausible. I guess." Cicely frowned. She

didn't like the idea that one of her sorority sisters could have set her up like that.

"It sounds more than plausible. The only question is, did you have anything to do with it?" Chase mumbled.

"Huh? You mean, did *you* have anything to do with it?"

"I didn't, and I don't think you did, either. I think we should call another truce." Chase held out his hand. "So how about the two of us form a truce *for real* this time. I feel somewhat comfortable stating that the election and my legacy were roadkill in the Sheila/Jonathan crash of love."

Cicely took his hand, and a charge of electricity coursed through her. It felt so sweet. She shook his hand and smiled.

"Good." Chase used his hold on her hand to pull her forward. "Because I have been waiting all night to do this." His head swooped down and his lips connected to hers.

She felt her lips heat almost immediately, and that heat covered her from head to toe as she opened her mouth to his kiss.

She thought for about a millisecond that she should be resisting this kiss, that she shouldn't be giving in so readily and so completely to Chase's very impressive mouth. Unfortunately, she thought that as her hands inched their way up his chest and onto his shoulders. Before she could mount up even the most basic rationale for why she needed to run away from the rum shack as fast as her size-seven feet could take her, she was already leaning into his muscular body, feeling the all-too-real impression of his need for her pressing against her. With one touch of his lips she was already in too far—and she didn't care.

Because this kiss…this kiss made that other kiss they'd shared in college seem like child's play. In that other kiss she saw stars. In this kiss, she could have sworn she was seeing universes, freaking galaxies. In that other kiss, she'd been a little nineteen-year-old, shocked that the big man on campus was showing her a hint of attention. But in this kiss, she was a grown-ass woman ready to show the big man a thing or two herself.

She pressed in farther and twirled her tongue in his mouth, using it like a heat-seeking missile. And every inch of him was hot. The electric shocks that she'd felt when she touched his hand felt like they were racing through her body. It made her feel so alive and invigorated. And his lips were like soft cushions that grounded the charge of the kiss and kept her from exploding or rocketing into the stratosphere.

His lips pressed and pulled and puckered in just the right way, at just the right time. All she could do to counter the impact was draw him farther into her,

Rivals in Paradise

devour everything he was giving her and delight in being able to do so. When his hands traveled down her back and landed on her behind, pulling her closer, she tried to get even closer still. She moved her hands from his neck, across his shoulders and down his muscular arms. She'd been thinking about touching those arms all evening. She felt her nipples tighten, and they strained through the material of her dress as if they were trying to get closer to him.

It was as if her nipples knew what the rest of her body seemed to be screaming.

He felt good.

Kissing him was too damn good. It was too much. She didn't know if she could take any more.

She pulled her tongue away, and he tightened his grip on her behind as he softly nipped her bottom lip, pulling it before he dived back into her mouth and found her tongue. Their tongues danced, and she was pretty sure she could have continued kissing him forever.

"Chase! They said you were back, but I didn't believe it. I just knew there was no way you'd set foot back on this island and not give me a call, cousin."

She managed to pull away from Chase at the sound of that male voice.

Chase pulled her back and held her close as he glared at his cousin for a moment. "I was going to call you, man. I've been busy. Tony, this is Cicely.

Cicely, this is my cousin Tony. He has always had the worst timing, and I see that hasn't changed." Chase let her go for a moment to embrace his cousin.

The two men hugged quickly before Tony turned to her.

"I can see why my cousin is so irritated with me right now. Hello, Cicely, did anyone ever tell you that you look exactly like the little girl from that Will Smith show, a grown-up version of her? I can't think of her name right now. But you look just like her."

Cicely shook her head, even though she knew exactly who he was talking about. People told her all the time that she and Tatyana Ali, who played the younger sister on *The Fresh Prince of Bel Air,* favored one another, but she didn't see the resemblance and she didn't encourage the comparisons. "Nope. Never."

"Well, you do." Tony held out his hand and she shook it. "Nice to meet you, Cicely. I'm going to go inside and get some food. I'm sure my cousin would like to get back to what he was doing."

They watched Tony head back into the rum shack, and Chase pulled her back into his arms. Thankfully, Tony's appearance had given her time to clear her head, and she was not going to allow a repeat of the kissing.

Chase traced her kiss-swollen lips with his thumb ever so gently and oh, so seductively. She took in a sharp breath and was already forgetting the intrusive, interrupting Tony and her vow not to kiss Chase again. His thumb felt amazing on her mouth, and it made her wonder what his other fingers could do to other parts of her body. She shivered at the thought.

"So, I guess all that, 'Ohhh, nooo! I don't even like Chase. I could never like Chase. Ohhh, nooo! I'm not attracted to that egomaniac, Chase' was just an act." Chase took creative license with her words as he mimicked her. His eyes were still hooded and still sexy, but his voice, the one that just a few minutes earlier could have talked her into even more daring public displays of affection, now had an edge to it that dripped of sarcasm.

Cicely's eyes narrowed as she ripped herself out of his arms and away from him and his stupid sexy thumb. "Do you mean you did all that kissing me just to try and prove some kind of point? Or to prove I was lying when I told your mother that there was nothing going on between us?"

"I'm saying you didn't have to be so quick and forceful and outright indignant with your outrage and denial! Really, Cicely, a brother has feelings." He playfully tried to pull her back into his arms.

She sidestepped him. He'd given her the wake-up call she needed. Never trust The Wolf.

Never, ever, ever, trust The Wolf....

He chuckled and placed his arm around her shoulder. "Don't get all salty now, Cicely. I didn't get salty when you acted like being in a relationship with me would be the equivalent of being in a relationship with the Attila the Hun."

"No, you didn't get mad. You just got even by once again using a kiss to make some kind of score."

Chase threw up his hands. "Oh, please, tell me we're not back on that again."

"No, we're not, because we have put it behind us and formed a truce. But I'm just making note of the fact that there seems to be a pattern to your kisses, Chase. That's all."

"Yes, and that pattern is, I really like kissing you and it really irritates me when you try and ignore or deny the attraction between us." Chase's voice got very deep and seductive.

Whoa. Wasn't expecting that kind of declaration....

Speechless, Cicely just swallowed and glanced around the rum shack's parking lot.

Chase shook his head. "Let's just go and enjoy the rest of the evening. And tomorrow, I'll take you on a real tour of the island. We didn't cover a lot tonight."

"Oh, you don't have to do that, Chase. I know you have family to connect with."

"I insist. Now, come on, I want to spend the rest

of the evening dancing with you and having fun. Do you think you can handle that, rival of mine?"

She smirked. "I can handle it. The real question is, can you handle it? You're a few years older. You might not be able to hang." She trotted off into the rum shack, looking back at him to catch his response.

"Oh, Cicely, you are a challenge, aren't you…" His voice trailed off, and she wasn't sure what to make of it.

Was it the competition for who could dance longer that caused that sultry expression to cross his face or some other challenge that had his jaw set and ready to win?

And did she stand a chance?

Chapter 7

Cicely must have tossed and turned the entire night after that scalding kiss with Chase. Her nipples seemed to be perpetually swollen. Her body remained piqued and ready to tumble over into bliss with just one touch from him. After she finally tumbled into a restless sleep, she found that it wasn't long before the alarm clock was waking her up. She dragged herself out of bed and managed to make herself look somewhat presentable, camouflaging the majority of the telltale sleep-deprivation signs with a little foundation. Needless to say, she wasn't all that pleased when she opened her door to find a well-rested Chase Yearwood ready to take her on a tour.

Cicely couldn't believe he appeared to be so unaffected by everything. She vividly remembered their brush with desire and the restless night of sleep it caused her. She was almost afraid to spend more time alone with him.

Yet he stood in her doorway, confident, strong, sexy and willful. He almost seemed to dare her with his very presence!

The daring nature of his stance must have jump-started something in her. Her competitive streak refused to be stifled. She decided to take him up on his dare. How much harm could a little sightseeing trip do, anyway?

She smiled at him and batted her eyelashes. "Good morning, Chase." She poured on demure like it was a new perfume.

"Morning, Cicely. Are you ready for your proper tour of Dahinda? I promise to do a better job of it this time. Today is all about you and showing you the best and brightest of Dahinda."

"Great, let me grab my purse and we can get started." Cicely walked over to the bed and made a show of bending to pick up her purse. She heard a slightly strangled sound coming from Chase's throat and thought maybe he wasn't as unaffected as he appeared to be.

The first stop on their tour of the island was the crystal caves known as Dahinda's Diamond Cove.

The subterranean caverns sparkled with what looked chandeliers of icicles dripping from the ceilings. The effect of the crystallized stone and the water underneath made walking through the underground cave an almost magical experience.

It was so captivating that Cicely found herself holding Chase's hand as they walked through.

"That was absolutely amazing," Cicely exclaimed as they exited the cavern.

"If you thought that was amazing, wait until you see what's up next," Chase said as they made their way to his sports car.

She happily took in the sights as they drove in his sporty rental. Growing up in Miami, she'd thought she was used to tropical beauty. But Dahinda was truly in a class all by itself. The palm trees, beautiful flowers and exotic-looking birds made her feel like she was in some kind of island fantasy. And, truth be told, the man driving her around and showing her the sights was playing a big part in that island fantasy. With the top down and the breeze blowing through her hair, she hardly had a care in the world until he pulled up in front of a sign that read "The Reptile Farm."

He parked the car and got out, but she didn't move.

He must have lost his mind.

That was the only reason she could think of to

explain why he thought it was okay to bring her to a place with a bunch of snakes.

He walked over and opened her door. She remained in the car.

Chivalry be damned!

She was not going into a reptile farm.

"What's wrong? You don't want to see one of the main highlights of Dahinda? Tourists love to come here and hold the snakes, pet the iguanas. You don't want to come in? They even serve the best grilled rattlesnake you've ever tasted. You have to cook it until it's well-done or it's still poisonous, but it's really good. And it's so cool to be able to say you actually ate rattlesnake."

She just stared at him.

Yep. He's crazy. He's lost his ever-loving mind. Poor thing.

He reached out his hand. "Come on, don't be scared. You'll like it. I promise I won't let any snakes get you."

"Chase, I'm not going in there. No how. No way. Forget about it. It ain't gonna happen." Cicely crossed her arms and smiled at him. "I hear there's a beautiful butterfly farm. We can certainly go and check that out."

"The butterfly farm? Seriously? That's so...girly. I don't think I've ever been to the butterfly farm."

Chase frowned. "You'll love the reptile farm. I'm telling you—"

"Seriously." Cicely cut him off with a smile. "I know I *won't* love it. I'd be willing to put money on that fact. I don't like snakes. I don't even like to see them on TV or read about them in books. The only way you would get me in that place is to drag me in there, and I'd dig in my heels and claw the dirt with my bare hands to keep you from doing that. So… butterflies?"

Chase shook his head and called her all kinds of girlie-girl names as he got back in the car and they drove off.

When they pulled up to the butterfly farm he grumbled as he opened her door, "And you better not tell a soul that I set foot in this place. Butterflies! Give me a break."

Chase had to admit the butterfly farm wasn't so bad. Sure, he would have preferred the reptiles. He used to love visiting the reptile farm the couple of times he had gone there as a kid.

The entire place was like a miniature tropical rain forest enclosed in mesh. There were so many trees and flowers and all kinds of exotic butterflies flying all over the place. And the joy on Cicely's face when she let one land on her finger was worth the chance that someone might have actually seen him there.

It was also very educational. They got to see the

various stages of a butterfly's life cycle, from egg to caterpillar to pupa to adult butterflies. It was rather amazing to see, even if it wasn't as cool as holding a snake in your hands.

Chase had to admit that doing the tourist thing and seeing his island home through Cicely's eyes made him value Dahinda even more. It really was a beautiful little island. In his mind, Dahinda always represented the very best that the Caribbean had to offer, and it was great to see someone else appreciating it.

After the butterflies, they decided to change into their swimwear and take in one of Dahinda's many beaches. He took her to one that not many tourists visited because he wanted to be able to enjoy her by himself for a while. As crazy as it seemed, he was genuinely starting to like Cicely Stevens.

Her aversion to reptiles aside, she was actually pretty cool.

Waiting for her to come out of the ladies' changing area, he contemplated what it meant that he was starting to let his guard down with her. It shouldn't have been that much of a risk.

He looked up and his mouth dropped open.

When she came out of the dressing room in her red bikini that gave new meaning to itsy-bitsy, he knew how much of a risk he was taking. He was in big trouble, and damn if he cared.

She was staring at his chest. Her eyes were wide, and her mouth was partially open. He reckoned he wasn't the only one in trouble. The only question was, what were they going to do about it?

He couldn't help it. He flexed just a little. He let his pecs move and silently thanked God that he spent time at the gym. When he saw her swallow and gulp, he sent up another note of thanks to God.

"You're really serious about this fling thing, huh? Because even if you weren't looking, I can promise you that you would find one wearing that bikini." He said his words slowly and deliberately, and her eyes moved from his chest to his face.

Her eyes narrowed, and she smiled her devilish little smile. He braced himself, because he knew his Cicely was up to no good when she smiled like that.

His Cicely?

She put her hands on her hips, striking a pose. "This old thing? You think I can land me a willing man in this little old thing?"

It was his turn to swallow and gulp when she did a spin and he got a look at that bikini from behind.

Thank God he'd had the foresight to take her to one of the more private beaches, because clearly this woman was trying to start a riot. He was torn between wrapping his towel around her, throwing her in the car, taking her home and making sweet love to her or finding a secluded spot on the beach and making sweet love to her.

The only thing he knew for certain was that if Cicely Stevens was serious about having a fling in Dahinda, she wasn't going to have it with anyone but him.

For some reason, submitting to the inevitable was a freeing thing. He realized that he could enjoy their time at the beach—indeed, enjoy the rest of the day—with Cicely without even touching her. Because before it was all over, before she stepped onto the plane to Miami, Cicely Stevens would be his.

He reached out his hand and she took it. He felt that shock of electricity that he always felt when he touched her, and this time it didn't throw him off at all. He welcomed it like a balm.

He smiled. "Yes, that little old thing. You're trying to cause riots."

He could have sworn he saw her blush.

"You know, Chase Yearwood, you're actually a pretty okay guy. I think I could *almost* like you." She stuck out her tongue.

He was pretty sure she did it to try and keep the confession that she liked him on a playful level. But he already knew the deal. Playtime was over. He just had to figure out when he was going to apprise her of that.

After spending the day seeing the island and hanging out with Chase, Cicely knew she was treading into some pretty dangerous territory. As she sat in her hotel room waiting for him to come pick her up for a night of dinner and dancing, she knew that even if they had decided to put their past differences and that student government election behind them, she was still in trouble. Her heart still remembered what happened the last time she let her guard down around The Wolf.

He was the one guy who made her forget the childhood vow she made when she watched her mother pine over the man who left her to die with no one there to care for her but her two kids and her mother-in-law. Cicely vowed to never let any man get close enough to hurt her. And most of the guys she dated never really had a chance to get close.

She had picked them for that reason. Her "type" had never really been her *type*. They were just safety nets for her heart.

But there was something about Chase. From the first time she'd met him in the student government office at FAMU and they got into their first disagreement about how the student fees allocated to student government could be used most efficiently, she knew he had the ability to get under her skin and possibly into her heart. And she'd made it her business—worked damned hard at it, even—to make sure they never agreed on anything. Except for that one kiss that nearly cost her the election and broke her heart, she'd survived her college experience with Chase almost unscathed.

But now…now…she was very close to running through hell with a pair of gasoline thongs on, and she was pretty sure she wouldn't come through this round with Chase unscathed.

Just thinking about how he looked in his purple-and-gold swim trunks almost had her breathless again.

That chest. Lord, that chest!

The man had a washboard stomach and pectorals that gave new meaning to the words "perfectly sculpted." And when he'd asked her to spread some sunscreen on his back?

Mercy.

She had to beg for mercy, because she didn't think she was going to be able to stop touching him, until he'd asked her if she wanted him to put some sunscreen on her back…

She would never really know or understand how she was able to make it off that beach and back to her hotel without making wild, passionate love to Chase Yearwood. All she could do was hope that whatever it was would get her through the rest of the night out with him.

The knock at the door startled her out of her reverie. She glanced down at her outfit and decided she didn't look bad. Her tangerine wrap-style dress was formfitting and stopped just about mid-thigh. She had paired the dress with some copper-colored leather strappy sandals, copper drop earrings and copper bangles. She went stockingless and just oiled up her legs. She had to admit the mid-thigh dress made it seem like her already-long legs were even longer.

Taking a deep breath, she opened the door, and for the umpteenth time that day she found herself staring speechlessly at Chase. He must have gotten the same wardrobe memo, because he had on a deep rust, short-sleeved silk shirt and some perfectly creased brown linen slacks. They looked very much like a couple about to have a sensuous night out on the town. And that was the problem....

They looked like a couple!

His eyes traveled down her legs and back up to her face. He gave a slow, easy, sexy grin. "So, are you ready to get a taste of Dahinda's nightlife?"

She was nowhere near ready for whatever Chase had in mind with his hooded eyes and his deep make-a-girl-weak voice. But she wasn't a punk, either. Stevens girls were tough!

She tilted her head and gave a half smile. "I'm ready. Are you?"

He held out his hand and she took it just to feel the warmth of that electric shock. She was starting to get used to it, welcome it, even. And that was the problem.

They drove to the restaurant in silence. She didn't trust herself to talk because she was pretty sure she would have said something stupid like, *Hey, Chase, wanna have a fling?*

So she twiddled her thumbs and let the island breeze relax her. She had come to the realization that she wasn't going to have an island fling after all. Because Chase Yearwood was the only man she wanted to have a fling with.

And she couldn't have a fling with him. She just couldn't.

When they reached the restaurant, she could hardly believe her eyes. It had everything. It was beautiful, romantic and right on the beach. They sat at a table that allowed them to look out onto the beach and ocean. The soft candlelight flickered off of the white tablecloths around the room. A steel-drum band played in the corner, and there was even a small dance floor. The restaurant exemplified upscale island chic.

"This is nice, Chase." Cicely finally trusted herself to say something.

"The food is good, too. Not as good as my mother's, but close." Chase smiled at her.

"Thank you so much for taking the time away from your family and friends to spend time with me and show me Dahinda. I really enjoyed today." She took a deep breath. "I think I can find my way around for the rest of the week. So you can spend time with your folks. And tell Margie I'm going to try my best to make it back to the rum shack before I leave."

It was for the best. She had to end this—whatever the hell was happening between her and Chase—before things got out of control.

Who was she kidding? Things were already out of control.

His eyes narrowed a little, and he just looked at her. He seemed to be processing something in his head. She really hoped that he was thinking things through and that he would come to the same conclusion that she had. Whatever was going on between them was a train wreck waiting to happen, and they needed their combined strength and resolve to stop it.

He nodded and took a sip of his drink, but he didn't respond to what she said. "You should try the conch fritters. We can get them as an appetizer. You have to have the curried coconut soup, too. All of the entrées are good. It's been a while since I've come here. But I'm sure the food is still excellent."

The waiter came and took their order, and she somehow restrained herself from ordering one of everything on the menu. When her food came and she finished everything, she really regretted her restraint. Everything was delicious. But because it was more upscale fare, the portions weren't nearly as big as those she'd had the night before at Margie's Rum Shack.

"That was delicious. But you're right, your mom's food is better. And she has better portions."

Chase laughed. "Come and dance with me, Cicely?" He stood and held out his hand.

She stood and took his hand.

The steel drums were playing so melodically. She was almost mesmerized by the beat and the man standing in front of her. He held her close as they swayed to the delicate island rhythm the steel-drum band created. Every cell and membrane in her body seemed to be screaming, *Him, you silly girl, it's him.*

But she blocked them out and told herself she'd just enjoy this one last night dancing in his arms, and she'd be able to get away before she had even more to lose.

He held her tight. "Tell me something, Cicely."

She cleared her throat. "What do you want to know, Chase?"

"If you're so determined to have an island fling, why won't you consider having one with me?" His voice was firm and strong, and the sound of it alone made her heart sputter.

But what he'd said? That was enough to send her into cardiac arrest.

She laughed what she hoped was a playful, sexy little laugh and not the shrill, frightened sound she heard in her own ears. "Because—"

She couldn't think of one blasted reason.

She looked up into his sexy, daring eyes.

Big. Big. Mistake.

He was looking at her like he wanted her, like he would give her an island fling she would never forget. And there was something else in his gaze. Something that she would never be brave enough to speculate about.

"Because...?" he repeated and waited for her to finish.

His arms felt so right, so incredibly right that it had to be wrong.

"Because you don't like me, Yearwood. And I—" *I could so easily fall in love with you.* "I don't like you, either. Why mess up a good thing?" She laughed again, and he just pulled her closer. She could feel his desire for her pressing against her and calling her a liar.

She swallowed.

"Is it because I'm not a nerd that you can wrap around your little finger?" He leaned down and whispered his words against her ear.

Yes, and so much more than that.

She knew what she had to do. She had to scare him off. Unfortunately, that meant showing a little bit of her vulnerability. But it would be worth it if it meant she could save herself from a broken heart.

Strategic honesty.

That was the way to go.

"It's because you're The Wolf, Chase, a bad boy… and you could probably break my heart and not miss a beat." She let out a deep breath as she realized the truth of her words.

He smiled ruefully. "You really think your heart would be the only one at risk?" He shook his head. "Fine, Cicely, I hope you find someone that you feel is safer for you. I'm not going to pressure you about this. But I'm also not going to help you find some lucky SOB so that you can give him what I want."

She felt that electric current racing through her even as a piece of her heart was already breaking. The pain let her know she was doing the right thing. So she just nodded as she continued to dance the night away in his arms.

Chapter 8

Chase sat at the bar in his mother's rum shack, feeling more than a little grumpy. He'd spent the entire day with his family, and it was wonderful, even if a huge part of him kept wondering what Cicely was doing and if she had found someone to have a fling with.

If he could have kicked his own ass for blowing things with her and not taking it slower, he would have. What was he thinking, asking her straight out why she didn't want to have a fling with him? It was the absolute wrong approach! Plus, he had sounded like a punk. He might as well have said, *Why don't you like me, Cicely? Please like me, Cicely. Please.*

What a chump!

No wonder she had given him the brush-off....

But he could tell that she was feeling him. He could tell by the way she melted in his arms, her pulse racing and her eyes fluttering...

He knew she felt the electricity, the chemistry between them. She was just scared. And she didn't want to risk her heart.

At least one of them was thinking, because he was ready to risk it all. And that wasn't a smart move.

No, it wasn't smart to risk his heart. Not where Cicely was concerned.

"So how come you didn't bring my girl Cicely back with you tonight? Where'd you take her last night?" Margie leaned on the bar and studied him with keen interest.

Rather than tell his mother that the last person he wanted to talk about was the woman who had been on his mind all day, the person everyone at the rum shack seemed to be asking for all day, he just shrugged.

Margie hit him on the arm with her cloth. "What kind of answer is that, Chase? You wait all these years to bring a woman here. You finally bring one and we all like her. And you had to go and mess it up!"

"Ma, not that it's any of your business..." He glanced up from the vodka tonic he was nursing and noted the dark squint of his mother's eye.

She used the cloth in her hand to slap him upside the head. "What do you mean, it's none of my business? I spent all day in labor to bring you in this world, and you can sit there and tell me what's my business and what's not my business? You're my only child, and I want you happy! You'll never settle down if you keep dating the kind of women who let you run all over them. Cicely is a nice girl. You can do a whole lot worse—and, come to think of it, you have."

"Your mother is right," Mr. Frank concurred. "You have to know how to tell a good woman when you see one."

"And she's cute, too. You two will make me some pretty grandbabies. She looks like that pretty little girl from *The Fresh Prince of Bel Air,* all grown up. So sweet and innocent." His mother smacked her cloth across his arm again. "Don't you hurt that sweet girl, Chase."

Chase ruffled at that.

Why was everyone worried about him hurting Cicely? What about Cicely hurting him? She could very well hurt him, too!

In fact, if he was honest, he would admit her unwillingness to have her little island fling with him had hurt him a lot more than he would ever let on.

"She don't look like no Hilary Banks," Mr. Frank grumbled.

"Not that one, the other one…Ashley," Margie said before rolling her eyes at Mr. Frank. "And shut up and mind your business, old man. You can't see I'm trying to have a conversation with my son?"

"Woman, I'm trying to help you. I thought you were talking about the pretty airheaded girl on the show. That's probably what he's used to dating, anyway."

Chase turned and stared at Mr. Frank, not sure if he should take the time to be insulted by the man's diss of his dating practices.

"Old man, shut up." Margie shook her head. "Anyway, Chase, you're not getting any younger. You're knocking on forty's door."

"I'm thirty-three, Ma."

"Like I said, knocking on forty's door. And women as smart and pretty as Cicely won't be coming around as easily. Mark my words, you'll regret letting this one go." Margie nodded in agreement with herself.

Chase sighed. "Okay, Ma, can we change the subject?"

"Sure." Margie smiled. "So, are you going to bring Cicely by tomorrow evening?"

Chase rolled his eyes.

"Oh never mind!" His mother said excitedly. "There's my girl! Chase, why'd you let me go on and on if you knew she was going to stop by here?"

She hit him with her cloth again. "Hey, Cicely, girl! How you doing? Come in and take a load off!"

Chase turned toward the door and almost fell out of his seat. There she was in his mother's rum shack looking absolutely stunning in a white sundress with big sterling-silver hoop earrings and bangles.

He knew he was staring at her. He almost wanted to pinch himself to make sure that she was really there.

Cicely smiled and walked over to the bar. "Hey, Margie! Hey, everyone!" The woman practically glowed.

"Chase." She nodded at him and quickly turned her attention back to the others.

He cleared his throat. "Cicely."

He took a sip of his vodka tonic and got up. He took her arm and led her over to the dance floor.

"Hey! What are you doing?" Cicely screeched as she let him lead her away.

He pulled her into his arms and started to move to the smooth R&B song that was playing in the background. He had no idea what song was playing, and he didn't care. The only thing he cared about was that she had shown up.

He had been thinking about her all day. He thought that he'd blown his chance with her. But she had shown up.

And if she really didn't want him to pursue her,

then she really shouldn't have done that. He had tried to do the right thing and let her call the shots and stay cocooned in her fear. But that would only have worked if she had stayed away.

Now…Now? Well, all bets were off.

He gazed down at her. That clear shimmer gloss thing she had going on with her lips seemed like it would be tasty. He decided to taste and see.

When his lips connected with hers, it felt amazing, damn near surreal. She immediately opened to his kiss, and his tongue didn't waste any time diving in.

Damn, her mouth was addictive. He wrapped his arms around her and held her closer as he all but devoured her mouth. He let his arms roam all over her lush, delectable curves.

It took everything inside of him to pull his lips away from hers and end the kiss. It was only the sound of clapping in the background that made him finally let her go. And even then, he kept her close to him. He looked around and his mom and her crew were clapping and whistling.

Cicely's brown face had just a hint of red on the cheeks.

"Chase—" she started.

"No," he interrupted her. "If you didn't want to be with me, Cicely, you should have stayed at your hotel where it was *safe*." He put extra emphasis on the word *safe,* since that was such a big deal for her. "I let you walk away from me last night, and I would have done the gentlemanly thing and respected your wishes. It would have killed me, but I really would have done it, Cicely."

He bent down, taking in her scent, and placed his forehead on hers. "But you came back here. You walked in that door looking like an angel, and now there's no going back, Cicely. There's no way in hell I'm going to let you find some clown on this island to have a fling with. That's not going to happen. Sorry. When we leave here tonight, you're coming to my place. And you might as well get your things from the hotel and check out. We've wasted too much damn time already."

"Are you finished?" Cicely twisted her lips to the side.

"Pretty much. If I think of anything else, I'll let you know."

"Cocky man! As I was going to say, before you interrupted me…" She paused with a saucy little grin on her face. "Chase, I want to take a risk and have a wildly passionate island fling with you. We'll just have some ground rules—namely, when I leave this island our fling will be over. No questions. No promises. No problems. These ground rules will help us keep things in prospective."

Chase bristled. Normally he would have loved

having an automatic out-clause written into a relationship. But for some reason, with Cicely it wasn't appealing to him at all.

"We don't need any ground rules, Cicely. What happened to your wanting to be spontaneous and do something wild and unplanned? Coming up with ground rules kind of goes against all of that, doesn't it?"

She sighed. "This is a deal breaker, Chase. If we can't agree on the ground rules, then we can't do this. No questions. No promises. No problems." She nibbled on her lip, and it made him want to kiss her again.

What was she so afraid of? They continued to sway with the music, but that question plagued him.

"Why do you feel like you need these ground rules so much? Are you afraid I'm going to turn into some kind of crazed stalker or something?" he joked as he spun her around. He gave her a peck on the lips when she faced him again. "I promise you, when you get tired of me I will respect your wishes and move on. *Of course* I'm going to try my best to make sure you don't get tired of me anytime soon. But—"

Cicely let out a deep, exasperated breath. It had been hard enough putting it all on the line, taking a cab over to the rum shack and admitting that she wanted to spend more time with him. She knew she was taking a huge chance with her heart. The ground rules had to be in place because they would remind her not to fall in love with this man.

She glanced up at his handsome face. He gazed at her with such earnest longing that she had to catch her breath. She'd already told him the other night that she needed to protect herself from getting hurt. How much of her soul did he want her to bare in order to have this fling?

What more did he want? Blood?

"That's not it, Chase. I need the ground rules in place because I…" *I could so very easily fall in love with you.*

She couldn't say that. No need to get carried away with the truth. "Because I think we need to be able to end things the way we started them, as friendly rivals." She smiled. "What we're experiencing here in Dahinda might be a fluke. It might be the island magic that is making us want each other so much. And make no mistake about it, I do want you.… But this is the only way I'm willing to go into this with you."

With his jaw set firmly, it appeared as if he were going to say no deal. Her nerves had her holding her breath. What would she do if he said no? She had already called on every ounce of strength and resolve she had in her to get dressed and take a cab from the hotel to Margie's. The entire ride over, she had to darn near bite her tongue to stop herself from telling the cabdriver to take her back to the hotel.

If he said no, where would she get the resolve and strength she would need to laugh it off and then spend an hour or two partying at the rum shack as if it didn't matter that he didn't want to have a fling with her?

"I don't like this, Cicely," he grumbled.

"We don't have to like it, Chase. We just have to respect the boundaries of it. That way, no one will get hurt and we can remain rivals-slash-friends." She smiled at him. "Come on, Yearwood. You know you want to say yes. There's unfinished business between us that we can settle before we go our separate ways."

"I don't want to place an expiration date on it, Cicely. We both live in Miami—"

"All the more reason for us to limit this. That way, neither one of us will have any expectations that we can simply bring what we start here back home."

"Are you seeing someone back home? Is that it? You have a man at home that you're here cheating on or something? Damn! I should have asked you that earlier." Chase shook his head in frustration.

"I don't have a man at home. I just broke up with my boyfriend. I had just given him a key to my place after dating him for a year, and I came home to find him in bed with another woman."

Chase's eyes narrowed. "You just broke up with a cheating boyfriend and you want me to be your *rebound* fling?" He said the word rebound as if it were a dirty word.

"No. Not really. I mean. I don't know. I don't think you'd really be a rebound fling proper, since technically I knew you way before I ever met him. And in a way we are settling old business from our kiss in college. Taking things further—"

"As far as we can take them in, what, four days? What if we need more time to explore?" Chase rolled his eyes and sneered. "And what if I'm not comfortable being your *rebound* guy?"

"Four days is all we have. And you aren't my rebound, Chase."

She placed her hand behind his neck and pulled his head down. Brushing her lips across his, she was surprised by how quickly he gave in to kissing her. Within seconds, he was devouring her mouth again. She figured her mouth would probably look like she'd had some kind of collagen injections by the time he was done with her. But it still pleased her that he seemed to want her so badly.

That had to be a good sign.

His hand trailed her arms and back, landing on her behind. He cupped her behind and squeezed.

Yes, that had to be a really good sign.

"Let's just say our goodbyes to your mom and talk about this at your place, if that's okay?"

"We'll see." Chase took her hand and they headed back to the bar. When he sat down at the bar, she followed his lead and sat down, too.

"Oh, oh, what happened? My son has his 'I didn't get my way' look on his face. Cicely from Miami, what did you do to my son when you all were over there dancing?" Margie had a big grin on her face, and it made Chase scowl even more.

Chase's reaction almost made Cicely reconsider her stance. It wasn't as if she thought she would ever get enough of Chase. That was the problem. She figured he would be tired of her long before she ever grew tired of him.

That was the way men like him operated, and they left a long line of broken hearts behind them to prove it.

Since she wasn't about to tell Margie that Chase was mad because he didn't want to have a short, no-strings-attached affair with her, she just shrugged her shoulders and smiled.

Margie picked up her cloth and popped Cicely on the arm. "Don't shrug your shoulders when I'm asking you a question."

Chase's eyes widened in outrage. "Ma, you can't just pop strangers with your cloth. There's nothing wrong with me. I'm fine," he grumbled.

"Cicely's not a stranger. She's practically family! And judging by how irritated she has your normally smooth and untouchable self, she's probably the only woman who can handle you." Margie smiled at Chase as he glowered.

Cicely giggled, which made Chase turn and narrow his eyes at her. "Margie, you are something else. Chase is fine. We're both fine. But I know I could use a plate of your excellent food. I haven't had anything else in Dahinda so far that compares."

"And you won't have anything else that compares. I'll fix you a plate." Margie glanced at her son. "How about you, Chase? You want something while I'm back there?"

"No, Ma. Just bring Cicely something. We're about to head out of here once she eats." He gave Cicely another poignant stare.

She could tell.

He had made his decision.

He was going to do it. Or do her, as it were…

Hooray!

He must have mulled over her terms and decided they were for the best.

Perfect.

That was exactly what she wanted.

Wasn't it?

Chapter 9

As she followed Chase into his home, so many things were going through her head. He had been pretty silent through the rest of their time at Margie's Rum Shack—so much so that she halfway expected him to take her back to the hotel instead of to his place.

But as soon as they entered his home, all of her second-guessing and wondering went out of the window. Chase was on her in a flash of steamy, scalding heat.

He pulled her into his arms as soon as the door closed and pressed her against the wall in the entryway. Their lips met, and the point of contact was electrifying. His kiss was so demanding, she knew that if he could have swallowed her whole he would have.

Just as his strong body pressed against hers, his lips pressed against her and into her, spilling forth a passion and desire that refused to be squelched. His tongue seemed to have a mind of its own as it traveled first around her lips and then through them, trailing her mouth and touching every erotic corner and crevice. The kiss was more than tasting and even more than devouring. This was some form of inhalation that had the opposite effect. The person doing the inhaling wasn't the one becoming inebriated. No, the one being inhaled was the one most impacted.

The drugging effect of Chase's kiss lulled her until she didn't know where he stopped and she began. She reached up and held his face in her caressing hands to try and still the storm, just a little, so that she could catch her breath. He responded by lifting her up onto the wall and cradling her on his strong, muscular thighs.

He pulled his mouth away from hers with so much effort you would have thought it almost killed him to do so.

He stared at her with a heat and desire that matched what was going on inside of her so completely, she had to close her eyes.

"Cicely, look at me."

She opened her eyes and faced the passion. She felt the fire.

"I want you to know that I am only agreeing to your terms under duress. And I reserve the right to revisit my agreement if I feel the need to."

She let her hands trail down from his face and hold on to his broad shoulders. With electric-fueled desire coursing through her body the way it was, the last thing she wanted to do was start some kind of haggling of terms with Chase.

"The ground rules are nonnegotiable, Chase." If her feet had been on the ground instead of dangling at the sides of his thighs, she probably would have stomped them for emphasis.

Chased placed his hands between the wall and her behind and pressed into her some more.

She felt him, hard and pulsing with need.

"My terms are nonnegotiable, too, Cicely. I'll agree to your terms because you have me so open right now, I would probably agree to anything. But I reserve the right to change my mind."

He pushed his hips forward, and the promise of what he had to offer made her rock her hips forward, too.

If only the barrier of their clothing weren't in the way.

He planted soft, teasing kisses down the side of her

face. "Take it or leave it, Cicely. It's the only way."
He pecked her lips once, twice. "Please, Cicely."

"Fine. We have a no-strings affair. No questions.
No promises. No problems. And you can reserve
the right to change your mind if you feel the need.
But—"

He cut her off with a kiss so potent it left her
breathless. His tongue was almost acrobatic in its
mission. It twirled and flipped and spun in her mouth
as if it were the star attraction in the greatest show
on earth.

She couldn't be outdone so early in the game, so
she moved her tongue slowly in and out of his mouth,
interrupting his pace, slowing it down but keeping
the heat of the kiss. She arched her back and moved
her hips, swiveling them and rocking them against
the hard press of his masculinity.

He met her, rocking his own hips as he groaned.

He let her slide down off of the wall. His eyes
were hooded in desire as he gazed at her. He lifted
the hem of her sundress, his hand inching it up her
thigh in a slow, seductive manner until he reached
the part of her inner thigh closest to her core. He let
his fingers move then. They moved her thong to the
side and then entered her, first one, then two, stroking
her and stirring up her desire. He moved his fingers
as skillfully as he had moved his tongue, and soon
she was moving her hips again. She moved in time

with his fingers, riding them until she cried out with a quick shuddering climax that took her by surprise.

Chase pulled her thong down, and somehow she found the coordination to step out of it. He pulled out a condom, unzipped his pants, freed himself and put the condom on. As he hiked up her sundress again, he lifted her from the floor and entered her so smoothly her gasp was delayed until she felt the fullness of all of him stretching her to her limits.

He held himself still, as if it would kill him to move. She used his stillness to get used to the breadth and depth of him.

"I'm apologizing ahead of time. Because this first time is going to be over much quicker than I want it to be." He gritted his teeth when she moved her hips and held her still.

The pulsing heat radiated from his body to hers, and she didn't know how he managed to remain still. He relaxed a little, but he still didn't move.

"Like I was saying…I have to take the edge off now. After this, I'm going to take my time and make love to you slowly, over and over and over until—"

"Oh, just do it already, Chase! Dang!" She managed to swivel her hips a little and she even bounced. The feel of him inside of her was addictive. She could have sworn that she felt each throb and pulse of his sex, swelling and contracting inside of her, on the verge of exploding.

He grabbed her hips and pulled out to the tip before thrusting back in. He used his muscular thighs to bounce her behind like a soccer ball, up, down and around before repeating his withdrawal and thrusting motion. He was moving so fast she barely had time to scream when another, bigger orgasm shot through her like lightning. The sound that came out of her mouth was a strangled cry that sounded much like an angry cat.

Chase didn't let her call of the wild stop his clever hips. He kept rocking her, rocking in her, faster and harder. Her back slid up and down the wall so swiftly she could have sworn she was wearing a new groove into it. There had to be a mark on the wall the very width and length of her torso, the way he had her going.

Even though it felt like forever as he continued to thrust and she continued to meet his thrusts, it was actually only a few minutes before he had joined her with his own release.

"Cicely. Cicely. Cicely. Cicely." He repeated her name over and over as he continued to stroke out the last of his orgasm.

Soon she found herself being lifted all the way into his arms as he slid out of her. She rested her head on his chest as he carried her, listening to his sure and steady heartbeat.

He took off her sundress when he stood her on

her feet and then picked her up again and placed her on the bed. She looked up into his sultry, seductive gaze and smiled.

"I'll be right back," was all he said as he left the room.

She assumed he was going to get rid of the protection, but she had no idea. The only thing she could think of was how satisfied she felt. She'd never felt so utterly and completely sated in all of her life.

She settled into the bed and thought it wasn't exactly as soft and cushy as it appeared. The plush white down comforter and humongous white pillows were a cloud-like surface covering a sturdy and firm bottom. It was just as comfortable as she'd thought it would be, though. She sighed at that thought as her eyes closed and she nestled her head into the nearest pillow.

When Chase came back into the room after removing the protection, he found Cicely fast asleep. The slow rise and fall of her chest and the restful half smile on her lips was almost enough to make him just want to get in the bed and hold her until he went to sleep also. *Almost*.

Cicely had awakened something in him that demanded more. And he had a feeling that even if he made love to her all night, or if they never left his bedroom for the next four days of her vacation, it still wouldn't be enough.

He had no idea why he had agreed to her foolish ground rules. Although, watching her stretch and curl back into her restful pose, looking absolutely tantalizing in her nude glory, he got a pretty good reminder of why he had agreed.

Moved by the sudden urge to touch her, to be joined with her, to make passionate love to her again, he removed his clothing and climbed into bed with her. His mouth immediately found her nipples. He took one in his mouth and sucked it in, alternating between sucking and nibbling softly, moving from one nipple to the other until her eyes fluttered open and she gazed at him.

"Oh…" She smiled and caressed his face.

He had never thought a woman would be able to spark such strong emotions in him just by smiling at him. But then, he'd only recently been the recipient of Cicely's smiles as opposed to her rolling eyes and frowns. And given the way his heart jump-started and his entire body became energized, he was going to have to keep this woman in smiles for a long time.

He let her nipple go and smiled back at her. "I told you the next time would be slow, and that we'd get started as soon as we were done with the first time." He captured her lips and kissed her awake, using his hands and that electric energy that sparked whenever they touched to finish waking her up. He caressed her breast, moved down to her belly and stroked her core until she wrapped her arms around him and rocked against him.

He closed his eyes as he felt her hot, sticky, sweet nectar spilling onto his hand.

Such a waste…

He kissed his way from her neck to her core, taking the time to get another nip and nibble of her nipples on the way down. Once he reached the spot where he wanted to stay awhile, he spread her legs and feasted.

Cicely's eyes opened wide then. She couldn't believe what Chase was doing to her with his oh-so-talented mouth.

She had never really been a fan of oral sex. She had always said it was overrated and pondered who really wanted some guy slobbering around down there.

But now…

Now she knew that those other guys just weren't doing it right. Chase had her torn between climbing the bed to get away from his plundering mouth and grabbing his head so that he would never ever be able to stop. *Ever.*

So she did some variation of both. She must have looked like a frantic mess. But she didn't care. How could she care when Chase was making her feel so damn good?

When the orgasm hit her, the only thing that kept her tethered to the bed was his strong hands holding her in place. She thought he might have taken pity on her then and stopped his skillful, mind-altering assault. But his mouth just kept working her until she found herself crying out with another release, shorter than the previous one but no less powerful.

Was it possible to die from pleasure overload? When she felt him finally stopping, she could only sigh.

Finally, he must have realized that she couldn't take any more.

She could hear him beside the bed, opening the nightstand, and then she heard plastic ripping and he was back.

"Slow this time, Cicely."

He inched inside of her, stretching her and filling her again, causing each of her already overstimulated nerve endings to pop and sizzle.

"Oh…" she sighed.

She couldn't really take any more. But she couldn't in good conscience turn down what he was offering.

When was the last time she'd felt anything this close to mind-blowing? Never. And where would she get a chance to have her world rocked again after this vacation was over? Nowhere.

So she needed to get while the getting was good.

She wrapped her legs around his waist and lifted her hips from the bed, meeting his thrusts with her own and trying to give as good as she got.

"I knew it would be this way between us, Cicely. It's so damn good, I can't even figure out how to tell you. So, I'll just show you."

Chase moved his hips in a slow, winding motion as he plunged deep and withdrew. She felt like he was marking out every vacant space inside of her, and those spaces were just satellites for the rest of her body—because each place his stroke hit caused other parts of her to react until she was feeling him deep in her heart.

Her heart raced with desire and devastation because she knew she would not leave this island the same way she had come.

She'd come thinking she was hurt after finding Isaac in her bed with another woman. But she knew that hurt would never match the hurt she was going to feel when her affair with Chase was over.

He kissed her neck, sucking and marking her. She turned her head, giving him full access as she rocked with him until another orgasm caused her to go still.

Her eyes were wide open, and her mouth opened to let out a scream of ultimate completion.

He captured her scream with a kiss, his tongue mimicking the sure and steady stroke of his hips.

She let her hands trace every delectable inch of his muscular frame that she could reach.

He felt amazing to touch.

He made her feel amazing.

When he lifted his mouth from hers and stared at her with that wonderful gleam of a man on a mission in his eyes, she couldn't help it. She went into overdrive. She moved on a mission of her own, and she wasn't going to be satisfied until she heard him screaming her name.

She lifted her hips, swiveled them and clenched her pelvis, giving him a loving embrace that made his surefire thrusts just a tad bit more erratic. She narrowed her eyes and concentrated on his handsome, masculine face as she lifted, swiveled and clenched, over and over and over.

"Cicely," he panted.

She smiled.

Close, but not quite.

She lifted, swiveled and clenched some more, but this time she added a clutch as she grabbed on to his behind, pulling him into her with every ounce of urgency she felt.

Unfortunately—or fortunately, depending on

how one looked at it—her actions were stirring up a reaction in both Chase and herself.

She was making him feel it. But she felt it, as well. And as it built and built and built until neither of them could contain it any longer, she found herself screaming out his name just as he screamed out hers.

It was only after several moments of perfect contentment that either one of them felt the desire to move. Chase flipped over on his back, taking her with him.

With her on top of him straddling his hips, he grinned. "Want to go for a ride?"

Chapter 10

After pretty much spending the next two days in Chase's house, only coming out occasionally for a few hours to visit Margie at her rum shack, and only really leaving the bedroom when they were in his house for things like food and cleanliness—which always led to prolonged, heated sex in the shower—Cicely awakened late in the evening of the second straight day in Chase's home, feeling the aftermath of their sexual gluttony.

The more you get the more you want.

There was absolutely no such thing as satisfaction. It was a myth created to lull fools insane enough to believe it. Or maybe it was for people who had never been loved to distraction in Chase's arms.

She rolled over and gave him a peck on the lips that turned into a prolonged kiss. It was around six in the evening, and her stomach was starting to growl for some of Margie's rice and peas.

She couldn't believe how close she'd gotten to Chase's mother. She felt like Margie's Rum Shack was home, and she was going to miss it and Dahinda more than anything. She knew she would never come back there. It would hurt too much to come back and know that she'd never be in Chase's arms again.

She playfully pulled away from him. "It's time for us to get up so that we can head over to Margie's. You know she'll tell both of us off and pop us upside the head with that dang cloth if we step up in there too late like we did last night. Plus, tonight is karaoke night, and I want to laugh at the people who can't sing."

He pulled her back and flipped her under him. "We don't have to go to the rum shack for that. I can't sing, and I'll sing off-key while I make love to you all night." He kissed her, melding his lips to hers in a sensuous and scandalous manner.

She moaned and wrapped her arm around his neck. It was only when her stomach made its growling noise again that he took a little pity on her and stopped.

"Okay, let's move this to the shower, then. We can finish up in there, and then I can go feed you and bring you right back here under me."

She laughed as he stood, picked her up and placed her over his shoulders.

"You better not drop me, Yearwood!" It was hard to sound threatening when she was so busy giggling.

Chase used the hand that wasn't holding her in place on his shoulder to slap her on the behind. "Be still, woman. I got this."

"Oooh, when you put me down, I'm going to get you."

Chase gave her behind another smack.

"Promises, promises." He placed her down in the spacious, doorless shower and turned on the water.

As the water fell over both of them he covered her mouth with a sweet, soul-stealing kiss, and she forgot all about getting back at him. The only thing she could think about was how good it felt.

He spun her around so that she was facing the marble-tiled wall with her hands flat against it. She felt him behind her reaching for the protection they decided to keep near the shower, just in case… Before she could turn to watch him cover himself, he was back and inside of her.

She turned her head, and he covered her lips as his hands covered hers and they rocked together underneath the water. She couldn't tell whether all the steam was coming from the shower or from their bodies.

His hips thrust up as his body pressed her closer to the tile. Before she knew it she was crying out with an orgasm that felt as if it had been ripped from her very soul.

God, I love this man was the only thing running through her mind as she felt like she was flung up toward the sky, only to come leisurely and flowingly back down to earth.

That was when she realized that she really meant those words, that it wasn't just lust and outstanding sex at play.

She really loved Chase Yearwood. God help her, she did.

He groaned his release just a few seconds later, still kissing her as if they shared the same lips and they would never part.

He removed the protection and walked back into the shower. They bathed one another lovingly, and Cicely's heart broke just a little bit more.

"Well, look what the cat drug through the door!" Margie greeted him and Cicely with open arms as they walked into the rum shack. She wasn't behind the counter for once, and she'd clearly been setting things up for the karaoke.

He hugged his mother and kissed her on the cheek and watched as Margie embraced Cicely. He still couldn't believe how easily Cicely seemed to fit in with everyone. And he really couldn't believe how wrong he had been about her all these years. There didn't seem to be a scandalous bone in her body.

He frowned as he thought about her stupid ground rules for their affair. He was certainly going to have to call in his right to renegotiate, because there was no way he was going to allow her to just walk out of his life in two days. He didn't think he'd ever get tired of her. So he wasn't letting her go. She would just have to deal with it.

He was Chase Yearwood, The Wolf, after all, and he didn't lose anything or anyone he really wanted.

He looked at Cicely and smiled. She smiled back and his heart lifted. Surely, she could be reasoned with. She didn't want what was building between them to end any more than he did. She was a rational woman. He would talk with her before she left and let her know that it was time for a change in terms.

Margie pulled Cicely with her. "Come on and help me set up the karaoke, girl. You can help me host if we start to get swamped."

Cicely looked back at Chase, and he waved at her as they went on their way.

He took a seat at the bar beside Mr. Frank. Mr. Frank shook his hand before turning back to his drink.

"This is the happiest I've seen your mother in a while, at least since your grandmother passed." Mr. Frank wasn't looking at anything or anyone in particular, but Chase could tell that the man was aiming for some serious talk.

"You have to try and make it home more often, son. I know she doesn't complain, but she misses you. She's so proud of you. Everyone in this bar knows your every accomplishment. And everyone in this bar knows that she is pleased as punch at the thought that you might finally be settling down."

"Well, I hope she isn't getting her hopes up too much. Cicely is going to take a little work."

"Yes, she seems a little skittish when it comes to you. But given your track record, can you blame her?" Mr. Frank chuckled. "Be patient, man. Don't bombard her with more than she can handle. Let her set the pace."

Chase frowned at that. If he let Cicely set the pace they would be over and done with in two days. And Mr. Frank's letting his mother set the pace hadn't gotten his mother down the aisle in twenty-something years.

Yeah. Right. He'd take Mr. Frank's dating advice with more than a little caution.

"I'll give her some room to set the pace, but I'll have to step in and navigate from time to time." *Like when I get her to renegotiate her silly ground rules.*

He was Chase Yearwood, and he didn't play by the rules. Rules were for suckers.

"I'm planning to ask your mother to marry me again." Mr. Frank had a big grin on his face that went against what one would expect from a man who had been turned down for marriage by the same woman more times than anyone could count. "If she says yes this time, we'll expect you and Cicely back for the wedding."

"If she says yes, then Cicely and I will definitely be back for the wedding." Chase didn't feel bad about making that promise because *if* his mother said yes to Mr. Frank then *anything* was indeed possible, including being able to get Cicely to extend their island fling into some kind of relationship.

"I know you don't think she's going to say yes." No one could accuse Mr. Frank of being slow, even if he didn't seem to get that Margie was probably never going to agree to marriage. He'd certainly called Chase on what he'd been thinking.

"But I'm telling you, I'm wearing her down. You could learn a thing or two from me, young man."

Chase laughed. "I don't doubt it, Mr. Frank. I don't doubt it at all."

"So, you gonna get up there and sing tonight? If you sing Cicely a love song, she might just get a little sweeter on you. I'm gonna get up there and dedicate a song to Margie tonight."

Oh, boy, please don't.

Chase knew for a fact that Mr. Frank was a worse

singer than he was. And that was saying a lot, because Chase knew he couldn't sing. Mr. Frank, on the other hand, was one of those folks who couldn't sing a lick but was totally clueless about this lack and jumped up to sing every chance he got.

Not a good look.

As people got up to sing, Chase hoped that Mr. Frank would forget about his desire to serenade Margie. He'd hate for the man to be embarrassed.

Chase was busy pondering Mr. Frank when he heard his mother saying words he knew he couldn't have heard properly.

"And next up we'll have my son and his girlfriend, Cicely, singing a duet that I picked out for them. This is an oldie but goodie, and I'm sure they'll have as much fun with it as we will have watching them."

Cicely's head spun around, and she backed away from the karaoke machine and Margie as if both had the plague.

"Oh, no, Margie. I told you I can't sing. I'm only here to laugh at other people who can't sing," Cicely said as she moved away.

"Come on, Cicely and Chase, it'll be fun. Give us something to remember you guys by," Margie coaxed.

Chase had never seen his mother look so happy and carefree. He liked seeing her like that. It made his heart light and made him get up from the bar and catch Cicely as she walked away.

He led her back over to the karaoke machine as she looked at him as if he were crazy. He kissed her on the cheek. "It'll be fun. And at least we can make fools of ourselves together."

"Oh, I think I'd much rather you make a fool of yourself and I sit and laugh at you while you do it," Cicely said with a nervous giggle.

Chase handed her a microphone and he took the other one. He turned to his mother. "Okay, we're here. Show us what you got, Ma."

His mother laughed. "Okay, singing Dynasty's 'Here I Am,' I present for your listening pleasure, Cicely and Chase."

Chase hadn't heard the song before. He was pretty sure it was way before his time. So he had to look at the little screen as he sang.

As the music started he noticed that Cicely had this deer-in-the-headlights expression on her face.

Great. He really hoped that she wouldn't freeze and she would able to carry her weight in this song. He glared at his mother when he got a good look at the lyrics. That woman would never quit, and she was eerily perceptive on top of all that!

The song was all about a man telling a woman he was ready and waiting for love and she was the one he wanted to give his love to. The woman's verses responded to the man's, telling him that even though she had been hurt in the past she would give him a chance if he were really serious about loving her.

Cicely could sing just a little better than he could. But by the time they started saying those lyrics to one another, it didn't matter. He knew he felt and meant every word, and he wondered if Cicely meant and felt them, too.

When they got to the second chorus, he chanced looking away from the screen and looked at Cicely. She was looking at him.

"Come get it, baby, here I am," she belted just slightly off-key.

"Let me be your lover, be your man," he crooned, more than a little off-key. He grinned at her as he finished.

He could only guess that they hadn't made complete fools of themselves because people were clapping and whistling. He pulled Cicely into his arms for a deep kiss. She kissed him back with so much passion, his mother had to make a show of pulling them apart.

"Okay, okay, you're taking up space and precious time. We have more people to hear tonight. The two of you shoo."

Chase hugged Cicely as they walked away. "You hungry? I can go in the back and make us some plates. I know my mother put you to work as soon as you got here."

"Yeah, food would be wonderful. I'll grab us a table."

He couldn't put his finger on it. But something seemed different about Cicely. He shrugged it off. He'd have the talk with her about extending their fling beyond Dahinda, and then things would be fine.

He wasn't worried. He'd get her to come around.

Cicely couldn't believe that Margie actually said yes to Mr. Frank's marriage proposal. Seeing the amount of love that Mr. Frank poured on Margie no matter what she said and knowing that the man had waited twenty-plus years for Margie to say yes just made her realize how pathetic her own situation was.

She was falling in love with a man who made a life mission out of changing women like he changed clothes, a man who up until a few days ago she'd fondly thought of as the last man on earth she would ever be foolish enough to kiss again, let alone have a hot island fling with.

But there they were, heading back to his place to pick up her things and a few items for him. They were going to spend the night in her hotel room because it was closer to his cousins' home, and Chase planned on spending some time with his cousins fishing in the morning before spending the rest of the day with her. She already knew she wouldn't be there when he came back.

She'd decided to leave a day early. It would have been too hard having him drop her at the airport, knowing that he'd be in Miami in a week and they couldn't see each other again. Her ground rules hadn't prevented her from getting a broken heart. But it would be even worse if she stayed any longer.

When they made it to her hotel room, he didn't waste any time pulling her into his arms and backing her toward the bed. They made quick work of their clothing, and soon Chase was kissing her all over her body.

She thought about the duet they had sung together at Margie's.

Although neither one of them could carry a tune even if it had a handle, she couldn't help smiling at the memory of Chase's voice crooning those words.

God, how she wished he'd meant them!

As he kissed her, his fingers coaxed her sex until she was writhing underneath him. She moaned into his mouth and ran her hands up and down his broad back. The feel of him under her hands made her want to feel him inside of her all the more.

Soon she was clutching his fingers in her sex. A small orgasm pulsed through her, causing her to arch her back in a silent plea for more. He chuckled.

"You ready for me, Cicely? Hmm? Let me know, babe."

"I need you, Chase. I *need* you." Her voice sounded raw and she was shocked by how much she didn't care that she wasn't just talking about the sex. Yes, she needed him to complete the sex act. But she needed him for so much more, and in her current state of mind, she didn't care who knew it.

"I need you, too, Cicely. I need you so much." He moved to protect them, and then he entered her.

She cried out as soon as his sex connected with hers. The impact was just that strong. She came with a force that stunned them both.

"Oh, God, babe, I'm not going to last. You're killing me, Cicely," he cried out as his release took him over the top.

He wrapped her in his arms after he got rid of the protection and laughed. "That has never happened to me before."

She smiled. She'd had lovers come quickly in the past but never after making her come just as quickly beforehand.

"Me, neither." She buried her head in his chest and inhaled. She knew she would remember the scent of him for as long as she lived.

"I won't wake you up before I leave in the morning. We'll get a really early start so that I can come back and spend the rest of my day and night making love to you before you leave on Saturday."

She didn't say anything. If she told him she was leaving in the morning as soon as he got up to go fishing with his cousins, he would have tried to talk her out of it.

She knew she was going to be leaving a big part of herself in Dahinda. But at least she'd gotten to turn her rival into a lover, a lover she would never forget.

Chapter 11

"Okay. What the hell are you still doing here, Isaac? I told you I didn't want to see you ever again. What part of that did you not understand? Did you have extra copies of my keys? I want every single copy, Isaac!"

Cicely glared at her ex. A part of her was beyond irritated that he had the nerve to be there. The other part of her was glad he was there. Leaving Dahinda had been the hardest and most painful thing she'd ever had to do, and it was good to have someone around to take it out on.

"I've waited here all week. I came back to try and talk to you last Sunday, thinking that if you had a couple of nights to cool down, you might be ready to listen to reason. But you weren't here, and you never came back. So I just wanted to be here when you came back…" Isaac had a kind of crazed glaze in his eyes that made her feel just a tad uncomfortable.

She moved closer to the door. "And why the hell would you want that?" Cicely snapped.

"I was hoping that once you had a minute to cool off you'd be able to see reason."

She made a project of turning her head to and fro, beside her and behind her.

"What are you looking around the room for?" Isaac asked in an irritated voice.

"I'm looking for Boo Boo the fool, because that's who you must think you're talking to, Isaac." Cicely shook her head. She couldn't believe the unmitigated gall of him showing up at her place and waiting for her to get back.

Isaac sighed and started pacing the floor. "No one said you were a fool, and no one is trying to play you. I was just hoping that you could find it in your heart to forgive me."

Cicely moved closer to the door and leaned against it.

"It's not about me forgiving you, Isaac. It's about the fact that you and I are over. I could forgive you and that would still be the case. In fact, I do forgive

you and I still don't want to be with you anymore."
Cicely sighed.

"Look, it just wasn't meant to be, and you obviously
knew that before I did. I should thank you, actually.
You weren't the man for me, and clearly, I wasn't the
woman for you. So could you just leave, please?"
She tried to talk in a calmer voice and mask her
irritation. Maybe a kindler, gentler approach would
have worked better with him? She doubted it, but she
was willing to try anything to get him to leave.

"You say that like you've found the man for you
or something like that." Isaac snapped his words out
viciously.

She thought of Chase.

Yeah. She had found the man for her.

Too bad she wasn't the woman for Chase.

It seemed like the only way she was going to get
Isaac out of her house was to be blunt and brutally
honest.

"I say that because you and I both know that what
we had wasn't mad, passionate love. I can't speak
for you, but I can speak for myself. I was settling for
less than real love when I was with you. And coming
home to find you in bed with another woman was
a pretty huge wake-up call. I don't want to settle
anymore." She crossed her arms and waited for him
to get a clue.

"And you wonder why I was in bed with another

woman? You are one coldhearted bitch, Cicely! How can you stand there and say some mess like that to me after all we've been to one another? You saying you didn't love me? What the hell? What the hell is that, Cicely?" Isaac was becoming increasingly irritated.

Cicely didn't think that he would do something stupid like hit her or anything. But she wasn't taking any chances.

"Listen, do I have to call my brother-in-law over here? It's over, Isaac. Over! Now, I'm going to run to the store and I want you gone when I get back. Just leave the key in my mailbox, okay? Please just be gone when I get back." Cicely turned quickly and left the apartment.

Her heart was racing. She wasn't sure if she had really needed to flee the apartment like that. But better safe than sorry....

She took out her cell phone and thought about calling her sister and brother-in-law so that Carlton could help her change the locks and be there in case Isaac got crazy or something. But she remembered that they were in New York City until Saturday. If only she had stayed with them, or maybe stayed in Dahinda until Saturday like she was supposed to...

She decided to call the twenty-four-hour locksmith instead and have them meet her at her place in an hour. That would give her some time to grab a few groceries, and hopefully Isaac would be gone by then.

When Chase got back to the hotel and found that Cicely had checked out, he wasn't too upset. He simply assumed that she had done what he had told her to do all along, moved her things to his place. It was only after he'd gone to his place and found it untouched that he realized she didn't have a key to his place. So she wouldn't have gone there. The only other logical place was his mother's rum shack. And when she wasn't there, it was time for Chase to face the obvious...

Cicely had skipped out on him.

Rather than get upset, he just smiled.

She really thought she was getting away with her little ground rules safely intact. Poor girl, she honestly believed that she was going to be the one to get the best of The Wolf twice in one lifetime.

It. Wasn't. Gonna. Happen.

He got on his cell phone, made some phone calls and pretty easily got her address and home phone number. She could run, but she couldn't hide.

When he returned to Miami he fully intended to continue seeing her. She did not get to call all the shots in their relationship when his feelings were involved, too.

And his feelings were involved. A lot. A whole lot

more than he was willing to admit or analyze, but he certainly wasn't going to let that keep him from full pursuit.

He gave her enough time to make it back to Miami and get settled before he called her to let her know exactly how he felt about her skipping town.

He waited as the phone rang and debated just how much of his irritation he was going to allow to surface. If she was apologetic enough, he might decide to go easy on her. But if she was still talking all that stuff about ground rules and the like, he'd have to take a firm line.

All of his debating went out of the window when a man answered her home phone.

"Hello," the male voice snapped.

Taken aback, Chase had to pause for a second before he queried, "Who is this?"

"Who the hell is this? You dialed my number, not the other way around."

"I'm looking for Cicely Stevens." Chase just knew he must have dialed the wrong number in his irritated state.

"She stepped out to run some errands. This is her man. Who is this?" The other man's voice picked up a healthy dose of bass.

Not one to be punked, Chase felt his chest puffing out as he asked, "You mean the man she just broke up with because she caught him in the bed with another woman? Would that be you?"

There was a fair amount of sputtering, and Chase could have sworn he could see the man's indignation through the phone lines.

"Don't you worry about what is going on between me and my woman. You just need to know that she and I will work out any problems we have between us. So, if she gave you any indication while she was mad that she was on the market, sorry, *partner,* you picked the wrong one."

Chase had to laugh at that. He didn't even know why he was wasting his time talking to that chump. Even if Cicely had suffered a momentary state of insanity and taken the chump back, he would be history as soon as Chase came back to town. Chase would make sure of that.

"Yeah, well, you just tell her Chase Yearwood called. And let her know that we will be finishing what we started in Dahinda when I get back to Miami in a week."

"Dahinda?"

"Yeah, Dahinda. Where she was all week with me, *partner.* Tell her I'll see her when I get back." Chase hung up the phone.

It was only after he'd hung up and his testosterone levels had gone back down to normal that he began to question if he'd done a smart thing by goading

Cicely's ex or man or whatever the chump was to her. He really hoped that the man didn't do anything stupid. Because he knew he would hunt the fool down if he laid a hand on Cicely.

He only knew that he was heading to Cicely's home as soon as he got off the plane next Saturday. Because ex or no ex, man or no man, Cicely Stevens had started something with him on this island, and he wasn't ready to just let it end because of some silly ground rules. He knew what he felt when he was with her, and he was willing to bet she'd run away because she was scared and she didn't want it to end any more than he did.

At least, that's what he was hoping....

When Cicely returned to her apartment with her groceries, the twenty-four hour locksmith guy was waiting for her. She was surprised to find her living room trashed and the cordless phone smashed and on the floor. She was so happy that she had had the foresight to leave when she noted that Isaac was getting unusually agitated.

She considered calling the police. But for the most part the damages to her living room weren't that bad. The hazelnut velvet sofa and loveseat were toppled, and chair pillows and throw pillows were tossed everywhere. The end tables were overturned and the coffee table was broken. The lamps where smashed, too.

The cost of a new end table, phone, lamps and locks was a small price to pay to get Isaac out of her life. If he came back and continued to be threatening she wouldn't hesitate to call the police on him. After this, she might consider going on a male-free sabbatical. If she had to worry about attracting losers like Isaac and she couldn't be with the man she had fallen head over heels in love with, then she might just as well be man-free.

She watched as the man changed her locks and contemplated her new man-free status.

She could do it.

She might not be able to do it for as long as it would take her to get over Chase, but she could do it for a little while. At least until the thought of loving someone didn't cause her chest to ache and make her want to cry....

"What's the matter with you? What's with the long face?" Margie slapped Chase's arm with her cloth.

He thought about not answering her, but he knew that would only earn him another smack with that damn cloth.

"You know, you really shouldn't be hitting people with that little cloth you walk around here wiping stuff down with. It's unsanitary, Ma. You could give somebody a rash or something." He made a show of rubbing the spot she'd just hit.

"Don't change the subject." Margie held her little

cloth weapon in a threatening manner, ready to strike again. "And you still haven't told me about Cicely and why she left early. Did the two of you have a fight or something?"

"No. We didn't have a fight. As far as I knew, everything was going fine with Cicely and me." Chase gave a half shrug. "But you can best believe when I get back to Miami I intend to find out why your new best friend got scared and ran. Plus she has to come with me to your wedding." Chase chuckled. "I told Mr. Frank I'd bring her, thinking there was no way in hell you'd say yes after all those years of saying no."

She slapped his arm with the cloth. "Stop getting smart, and stop trying to change the subject."

"I'm not trying to change the subject, Ma. It's complicated."

"Please." Margie sucked her teeth. "How complicated could it possibly be? Either the two of you love one another and want to be together or you don't. It's not rocket science."

"Tell that to Mr. Frank— Ouch!" This time the cloth stung when she hit him with it.

The first chance he got to hide all of her little terry cloth towels he was going to do it. The woman had to be stopped from terrorizing the world.

"You always were such a smartass." Margie pointed her finger at him and was reminded immediately of what people said about pointing fingers. His mother had fingers pointing back at her, because he had come by his smart mouth *very* honestly.

"If I didn't like Cicely so much, I might say it serves you right that the one girl you want to get serious with is the one playing hard to get." Margie tapped her lip in contemplation.

Chase frowned. "Who said I wanted to get serious? I just want to give us time to explore what we can be. She would rather put a timetable on things and let what we have end on this island because she's too afraid to risk her heart for more than a fling."

"She isn't the only one who is scared and doesn't want to risk her heart." Margie gave him a knowing look that made him feel like he was still a kid and he'd gotten caught trying to steal an extra cookie.

"You think because you say you want to expand the expiration date of your 'island fling' beyond your time on the island that you are somehow not afraid? What about your desire to win all the time no matter what?" Margie fired her questions like she was the police or something.

Chase rolled his eyes. *Not the you-have-to-win-all-the-time-and-there-is-something-really-wrong-with-that speech. Please, Ma, anything but that.* He knew better than to say that out loud, though, because his mother would have smacked him with that cloth hard enough to leave a mark and he would have gotten an even longer speech. And she would have followed that speech with the it-took-me-a-whole-day-of-labor-to-bring-you-in-this-world-so-I-get-a-say-in-your-life-forever speech.

"Sometimes you have to risk everything even when you know you might lose. That's when it matters the most. When you know you don't stand a chance, but you go all out anyway because your heart and soul won't let you rest unless you do. That is why I finally said yes to Frank, even though I'm more than comfortable keeping our relationship the same as it has been.

"He's my man and I'm his woman, and since it wasn't broke, I couldn't see the point in bothering with it. But he kept asking me, all the while expecting that I'd turn him down again. He never gave up on me, even though I gave him *no* reason to expect that I'd change. Do you see yourself doing that for Cicely, as much as you hate to lose? Can you see going all out and pursuing her like a man intent on making her his for real instead of a man looking to continue a fling until it's flung? That's living without fear, my hardheaded, stubborn son who is the love of my life. Can you, or do you, love Cicely like that, without fear of losing?"

Chase squinted his eyes. His mother had laid down some heaviness, and he really had to ponder her words.

Could he lay it all on the line knowing that he didn't stand a chance? He didn't know. He'd always approached everything without a care about losing, because he'd always won and he didn't expect that to change.

With Cicely, he'd already seen that he could lose to her when she beat him in college. If she really didn't want him, would he have the tenacity to keep trying to make her see that he was the one and only man for her, knowing that she might never see it?

He wasn't sure if he could. But he was damn sure going to try.

Chapter 12

Feeling like you peaked in college, finding the man of your dreams, only having a brief island fling with said man of your dreams and wondering if you should take out a restraining order on your formerly quiet and nice nerdy ex-boyfriend instead of just changing your number like you opted to do was enough to make a girl go for the Krispy Kreme doughnuts *and* the Chunky Monkey ice cream.

Cicely wondered if she should take her brother-in-law up on his offer. Working for Harrington Enterprise wouldn't have been that bad. The import-export business of dealing with cement and oil refineries was probably more interesting than she had imagined.... *Not.*

At least she wouldn't have to worry about Leonard Stone sabotaging her and belittling her left and right.

After a week of dealing with her jerk of a boss, ignoring Isaac's apologetic phone messages and not hearing a word from Chase, her life was just as crappy as it had been before she'd taken the trip to Dahinda that was supposed to help her get her groove back.

Granted, she shouldn't have expected to hear anything from Chase since she hadn't left him any of her contact information....

But a small part of her was hoping.

So, instead of having a Saturday night out with her girls, or hanging out with her sister, niece and nephews or even spending some time with Gran, she was in her condo. Her hair was up in a haphazard ponytail and she was wearing a pair of ripped-up sweats and an old FAMU T-shirt, eating a pint of Chunky Monkey ice cream and watching a marathon of old romantic comedies.

Seriously, why couldn't her life be like Julia Roberts's or Sandra Bullock's or Meg Ryan's? Well, maybe not their lives, exactly, since the actresses were probably as unlucky in love in their real lives as she was. But definitely the characters they played in those little movies Latonya had gotten her hooked on.

A perfect job—well, with the exception of Vivian Ward, Julia's hooker with a heart of gold in *Pretty Woman*—a perfect man to sweep her off her feet and a perfect life…

Was that really too much to ask for? Really?

She was just at her favorite part of *Notting Hill,* where Julia's Anna tells Hugh Grant's William that she's just a girl standing in front of a boy asking him to love her. That part always guaranteed a good cry, and she needed a good excuse to cry, otherwise it would seem like she was sitting in raggedy sweats, stuffing her face, moping and crying over Chase Yearwood.

And she was not doing that! She was just in a little mood, that was all, and it would pass soon.

There was a knock at the door and then a prolonged press of the bell.

She huffed and put the movie on pause. If Isaac had taken to showing up at her door now that she had changed her number, she was going to call the police and take out that restraining order.

She looked through her peephole, and what she saw there shocked her to her core. Chase was leaning against her door like he didn't have a care in the world. How he'd managed to get her address and why was he showing up at her place took second place in the line of questions running through her head. Those sensible questions had no billing with her.

No, the top thing on her mind was, *Do I look presentable enough for him to see me?*

"One second." She took the scrunchie out of her hair and gave her do a quick finger toss. She looked down at what had formerly been her favorite pair of orange sweats but had suddenly morphed into a fashion-don't now that Chase was going to see her in them looking like a slouch.

She opened the door, and her breath caught in her throat. Chase pulled her into his arms and kissed her, sending her world into the stratosphere and making a pretty shitty week all of a sudden *the best week ever.*

Chase knew he should have said something first before he just attacked Cicely with his lips. But seeing her there looking so adorable and clearly shocked to see him, made him want to kiss her and shock her even more. The more he tasted her the more intense his feelings became.

She'd left him, left him with out a care or a way to contact her.

She'd left him as if it had been the easiest thing in the world to do and gone back to her cheating ex-boyfriend.

His lips stopped mid-kiss and he pulled away. He touched her face, stroking and caressing it lovingly as all of the questions he wanted to ask her bounced around in his head.

"Is your *man* here? You said the two of you broke up. But he answered your phone when I called you and staked his claim…" He took a deep breath, but he didn't take his hand off of her pretty face.

"My man? When did you call me? I don't have a man. No man should have answered my phone. And I just got my phone number changed because my ex wouldn't stop calling. He was still here when I came back from Dahinda. So I had to make him leave, and then I had the locks changed in case he had more copies of the keys. I left to go to the store while I waited for the twenty-four hour locksmith to show up when it seemed like he was getting a little extra upset about the breakup. When I came back he had trashed the place and smashed my phone."

Chase nodded and walked into her condo. He probably should have waited for an invite, but…oh, well…

"Sorry about that. He probably decided to wreck the place after talking with me. He didn't seem to like what I had to say. And for the record, you *do* have a man. I'm your man." He gave her a pointed stare that he really hoped she wouldn't argue with. They had wasted an entire week apart. That was too damn long. "And we are renegotiating your ground rules. I'm not letting you go."

He walked over to her sofa and sat down. A movie was on pause, and a bunch of DVD jackets from other movies were all over the place. *You've Got Mail, When Harry Met Sally, Sleepless in Seattle, Runaway Bride, How to Lose A Guy in Ten Days* and a bunch of other chick flicks were scattered all around.

Someone must be in an interesting mood.

He sat down on the sofa and picked up the empty pint of Chunky Monkey ice cream that was on the end table.

Yes, someone must be in a really interesting mood. Regret, maybe?

He turned and saw that she was kind of stuck in the same spot. She hadn't moved. "Are you going to stand there all night?" he asked.

"No, I'm just wondering what you're doing here, Chase. I thought we agreed that we'd have an island fling. No questions. No promises. No problems."

"And I told you I was agreeing to that mess under duress and I retained my right to change my mind. I've changed my mind. Come sit down by me, Cicely. I've missed you."

Her eyes widened even more, but she came and sat down next to him.

His heart was beating like he'd just run a marathon. He didn't know if he was truly ready to put everything on the line just for Cicely to tell him no. He wanted so much more than to just continue their island fling.

He wanted to build a relationship with her. The truth was, he had finally found a woman that he wanted to be his wife, to have his children. And he didn't think he could take it if she turned him down once he put his entire heart on the line.

His mother was right. He was scared to lose, especially when it mattered. He now realized why the student government presidential election had plagued him for all those years. It wasn't losing the election that had hurt him. It was losing all of the possibility sparked by that one kiss with Cicely that had hurt the most.

"How did you get here?" Cicely asked. She had an expression on her face that was a mix between confused and irritated. "You're not supposed to be here, Chase! Why do you think people have boundaries? Just for you to stomp all over them whenever you like?"

The shock was wearing off, and she clearly had her guard up.

Chase turned to face her, pulled her into his arms and kissed her. She needed an outlet for all that fire, and he was more than willing to provide one.

Their heated passion took over in seconds, and she kissed him back instead of questioning his motives. He decided he would do that before he answered any of her questions, especially the ones where she had an attitude.

"You don't get to just put up boundaries when there are two people involved, Cicely. It's unfair. I'm not going to be Mr. Frank and let you string me along for twenty-something years just because you think it's some kind of test of how much I care. You ran this time and I found you, but you can't keep running just because, Cicely. You're not the only one who is scared."

He realized he had revealed way more than he'd intended, but he couldn't stop himself. His stomach felt queasy, his throat was dry and his palms were sweating. He felt like he was walking a tightrope without a safety net. He usually enjoyed the thrill of risk taking. It lit fire to his blood. But risking things like money, property, status and anything else that didn't involve feelings was pretty easy for him. This kind of risk was not.

This must be what it feels like to go for broke.... He didn't like the feeling at all.

"It was hard enough to leave Dahinda—"

"Didn't seem like it was hard to me. You just left me there without a word or a backward glance," Chase interrupted.

"It was hard, Chase! And now you're here and I don't think I'll be able to walk away from you again." She nibbled her upper lip and shook her head. "Don't you get it, Yearwood?"

He traced her lips with his tongue deliberately,

as though he had all the time in the world. And then he slowly snaked his tongue through her lips and touched hers ever so softly. It only took that moment of contact for her tongue to wake up and start dueling with his. Their tongues danced for several minutes before he pulled away.

"Good. I'm glad it will be hard for you to walk away again. It should always be hard for either one of us to walk away." He kissed her again before standing. He held out his hand. "Can we please go to your bedroom so that I can show you how much I've missed you?"

She took about a second to contemplate before she followed him.

Cicely let The Wolf into her bedroom. If Chase was determined to carry on their affair beyond the beautiful blue skies and teal waters of Dahinda, then she'd just have to put on her big-girl panties—*or* take them off, in this case—and have him for as long as it lasted.

She slowly undressed him, taking her time to appreciate every bulge and muscle she'd thought she would never see again. His skin beckoned for a kiss and then a lick. So she kissed and licked every area she stripped. Soon he was standing in front of her, naked in all his beautiful male glory. His manhood jutted forth like a very long, very sturdy rod. She dropped to her knees and took his shaft in her mouth, kissing and licking it the way she had the various other parts of his body.

Just as she had wondered when he was giving her oral pleasure on the island, she again pondered how she could have gotten it all so very wrong.

Fellatio wasn't overrated at all. It was her new favorite thing, both the giving and receiving.

When she had driven him almost to the point of no return, he pulled out of her mouth with a gasp. He pulled her up and made quick work of her sweats and FAMU T-shirt.

"Hey, be careful with the threads, dude. They're vintage," she joked when he yanked down her incredibly torn sweatpants.

He laughed, grabbed a condom from his pants on the floor and covered himself. When he came back to her, he tried to walk her backward to the bed. But she flipped the script, turned him around and walked him backward instead. She straddled him once she got him where she wanted him and eased down his shaft like she was coming home.

It felt wonderful.

She moved her hips up and down, riding him like her name was Annie Oakley. She bent down and continued tracing the contours of his chest with her tongue as she rode him. He grabbed her hips and bucked upward, proving to be a pretty wild stallion indeed. She clutched her inner thighs as her inner walls clutched him and held on for the ride of her life.

They both rode until they found completion in sated bliss and then rode some more. They spent all day Sunday in her bed. And when he left, telling her that he would be back on Monday evening after work, she was okay with that. She was going to ride this ride for as long as it lasted and worry about the consequences later.

Chapter 13

"Wait until you meet the guy they hired to head up Mergers and Acquisitions. I know you threw your hat in the ring for that position, Cicely. But you barely do a decent job without me riding you 24/7 here in Finance. This guy they hired, due to my recommendation, of course—" Leonard Stone took a breather to puff out his already overstuffed chest before finishing "—is a real predator in the business world. He's not afraid to do what it takes to win."

Cicely rolled her eyes as she listened to her division head go on and on about the new hire. He delighted in rubbing her nose in the fact that someone else had gotten the position she'd wanted so very badly.

She wanted to do him bodily harm, and she despised him for bringing out this evil part of her. She could have gone her entire life without even knowing that something like that existed in her. Someone who could stab Leonard Stone in the eye with her number-two pencil and laugh crazily lived inside of her, and she had to keep that person chained and subdued, or else…

They were sitting in the conference room waiting for the president of Mainstay to come in and introduce the new boy wonder. The person's identity had been kept hush-hush, but now everyone was going to meet the man.

Cicely couldn't care less. Any friend of Leonard's was an enemy of hers. That was for certain. She couldn't care less if the man walked on water and turned said water into wine. She was not going to like him. Period.

She practiced zoning Leonard out as he went on and on about the last report she'd written that apparently wasn't up to his standards.

Big. Surprise.

She tried not to hate people, but she was starting to hate Leonard Stone.

Who was she kidding? She despised the man. She didn't know if she could despise anyone more until she saw Chase Yearwood walking into the conference room with the president of Mainstay, Ron Samuels.

Chase had taken her job.

Chase was a friend of Leonard's.

Chase had made love to her like no one ever had, shown her his softer side and made her fall in love with him.

And Chase had taken her job.

The jerk!

Oh, sure, Chase seemed shocked at seeing her there. But one look at Leonard Stone's smug face told her that somehow he and Chase must have been in cahoots. Leonard was one step away from saying, *Na-na-na-na-na.* And she just knew that's what he was thinking.

Woosah.

She tried to calm the crazy, pencil-wielding maniac inside of her, but it was extra hard. There were two people she wanted to puncture with her trusty number two now....

Everything went by in a blur. The introductions, Ron Samuels reciting Chase's impressive resume, all of it might as well have been *blah, blah, blah* as far as Cicely was concerned.

Her heart felt as if someone had taken a butcher knife to it. She just knew her chest had to be bloody and her heart must have been spurting all over the place, because that's what it felt like. She couldn't get over the hurt and betrayal she felt.

Was this or was this not the same man who had

just made love to her all day Sunday? Had he or had he not begged her to continue their fling—which he was now calling a "relationship," by the way…

When the traitor finally made his way to her division, she had resolved that she would play it cool in the workplace. But the first chance she got outside of work, it was going to be on!

"Hi, Cicely. I didn't know you worked for Mainstay." Chase glared at Leonard. "That's something you could have told me, Leonard."

Leonard laughed his boisterous, annoying "ah ha ha ha, ah ha ha ha" that sounded like a jacked-up Santa who didn't know his lines. She hated Leonard's laugh almost as much as she hated Leonard.

"So, you're trying to tell me that you didn't know I worked here?" Cicely seethed. "Next thing you'll be saying is you didn't know that I was also in the running for your job until the company found out that could get this whiz-kid interloper."

Chase's eyes narrowed.

Leonard smiled. "Almost karmic, isn't it? Except karma had nothing to do with it." Leonard walked away, looking a little too pleased with himself.

Chase sighed. "I honestly didn't know, Cicely. We didn't talk about work in Dahinda. And Leonard didn't let on that you worked here. He certainly didn't tell me that you also wanted this job. If he had, I can't say for sure it would have made a difference when I first applied, because a few weeks ago I still held a grudge against you and it would have made my big ego feel vindicated to know I beat you out of something you wanted. But now I feel horrible."

"Yeah, right, Chase. Listen, I don't believe in fraternizing with my colleagues and especially not my superiors…so, needless to say, anything we agreed on continuing yesterday is null and void today."

"The hell it is, Cicely. You don't get to just decide that—"

"The hell I don't!" She narrowed her eyes at him in disgust. "Careful, Mr. Yearwood, you don't want to pick up a harassment suit on your first day. Stay the hell away from me." Cicely walked away with her head held high even though her heart was broken.

Chase didn't know what to make of the fact that Cicely worked at Mainstay and Leonard hadn't thought it was important to share that tidbit of information. Leonard had probably been going for the shock factor. Especially since he knew how much Chase had hated losing that election to Cicely years ago. But Leonard would have been the one in shock if he had known just how far past all of that nonsense Chase and Cicely had moved.

Only to end up further back than they had started! Chase knew in his heart that Cicely had meant every word she'd uttered to him in the conference room on his first day. That first workday had kept him too busy to go and talk with her again. He'd had a whole new company and a whole new way of doing things to process. But he did try to talk to her later that evening and again and again every day since.

When he tried to call her she didn't answer.

When he dropped by she refused to answer the door.

He knew she was hurting because he could feel it. But he was hurting, too. Being without her was killing his spirit.

As he sat in his office wondering if she would make good on her threat to file a sexual harassment suit if he didn't leave her alone, Leonard came waltzing in.

"So, I thought I'd give you a little time to get the lay of the land and get over the shock of seeing Cicely here. I thought that would get you good, seeing her. But don't worry. She's on her way out of here, man. As soon as I can manage it, I'm axing her behind. I'm just biding time since she's worked here for a while."

Chase wanted to punch that smug look off of Leonard's face. But he decided to let the fool cut enough rope to hang himself. As hard as it was to listen to Leonard, he just let the man talk.

Chase leaned back in his chair and kicked his feet up on his desk. "I was rather surprised to see her, and even more surprised that you would think that I didn't need to know that little piece of information before I took a job here."

"That's the beauty of it. You can help me get rid of her and pay her back for wiping the floor with you during that election. Just think of her little prissy know-it-all self out of a job in her thirties, in this economy. It would be a dish served cold for sure." Leonard took a seat without being offered one.

Chase tried to keep himself calm, but the venom in Leonard's voice was taking him to a place of no return. He cleared his throat and loosened the knot in his tie a little. It helped stop him from pummeling Leonard for the moment. He needed more information. Leonard seemed to have far too much anger where Cicely was concerned.

"Tell me something, Leonard, what did Cicely ever do to you? Why do you dislike her so much?"

"I don't dislike her. I hate her. First, she thought she was too cute to give a brother the time of day in college. I asked her out and she turned me down flat. But then she used to make goo-goo eyes over you, left and right, when she thought no one was looking. I could tell she had a thing for you even then. She probably still does, I caught her watching you the other day all longingly when she thought no one was watching her. I bet it's killing her having you here!

"Do you know she didn't even remember me at first when I came to work here? Me? After all that time we all spent in the SGA office, she had the nerve to have to be reminded of who I was. But she remembered you just fine, didn't she. I always knew she had a thing for you. And that night when you were feeling her up and kissing her in the SGA office… man, that was something. I thought the two of you were going to take it all the way. I was glad I had my camera. But she stopped after all that teasing."

Chase stood up then. "You took the picture of us kissing?" He walked around the desk and stood by Leonard's chair.

Leonard sprang up and backed away, clearly rethinking what he had, in his bitter tirade about Cicely, over-shared. "Okay, listen…you're going to find this sort of funny. Yes, I took the picture of the two of you kissing. I don't know why I took it. But after I took it, I figured it would be a way to possibly snag the election for myself. I figured once it was leaked, it would ruin both of your chances and I could swoop in as the write-in. So, you see, Cicely ruined the election for me, as well." Leonard backed up, inching toward the door.

It was all Chase could do not to punch the man. He did follow his every step, though. And his hands did find their way around Leonard's neck quicker than a flash. Before he knew it, he had Leonard jacked up against his office door.

"Hey, man, it was just a college election," Leonard

sputtered as his feet dangled in the air. "This is unprofessional, man! I could get you fired for this or press charges. You need to watch it! Sheesh! I can't believe you're tripping like this."

Chase sneered, feeling more like a wolf than he had ever felt in his life. The need for blood raced through him.

"Let me get this clear. Were you trying to use me in your sick little vendetta against Cicely?" Chase gritted his teeth, and he still didn't let go of Leonard's neck or let him down from the wall.

"Yes...I mean, no...I mean, I don't know, man..." Leonard's answer changed each time Chase's grip tightened on his neck.

"Okay. You seem confused. Let me clear this up for you. You are going to let go of this little vendetta of yours. Because Cicely Stevens is off-limits. I will go to any length to protect people who are important to me. And Cicely is the most important person in the world to me. She's the woman I love. And if you so much as look at her sideways, you don't even want to know what I'll do to you."

Chase let Leonard slide down from the door. He straightened his tie and started walking toward his desk. "Get the hell out of my office, Leonard. And do try to stay away from me. It would be in your best interest."

Leonard gained a little more courage once his

feet were on the ground and the door was partially opened. "You stay the hell away from me, too, Yearwood. Based on our former friendship, I won't press charges on your ass. But for the record, we are no longer friends!"

Chase narrowed his eyes and started walking back toward Leonard. "Why are you still in my office?"

Leonard made haste getting out of there.

Cicely sat in her office, stunned. She had gone looking for Leonard and was more than a little irritated to have to hunt him down in Chase's office, of all places.

She so did not want to have to see Chase with all his I'm-sorry-I-didn't-know crap. He'd been calling her and trying to see her, but she'd been doing a pretty good job of not seeing him. It hurt too much to see him, and now she really couldn't have him because he was in league with The Evil One.

She didn't know what she had done to Leonard to make him hate her so much, but she did know that if Chase had ever really cared anything for her, he wouldn't be a friend to a person who despised her to the degree that Leonard did.

She walked up to Chase's office. She could hear Leonard's big, ugly, braggadocio voice clear into the hall. And what she heard shocked her to her core. Leonard's vicious hatred spilling forth to a clearly listening and willing participant—Chase:

That's the beauty of it. You can help me get rid of her and pay her back for wiping the floor with you during that election. Just think of her little prissy know-it-all self out of a job in her thirties, in this economy. It would be a dish served cold for sure.

That was enough to seal the deal for her. Chase was in league with the devil. It was only after she got back to her office that she realized she was giving both of those pigs too much leeway. She wasn't going to take any more of Leonard's crap, and she was going to confront Chase about his part in this. The least he owed her was an explanation.

She went back to Chase's office after contemplating what to do. The workplace was not the place for their confrontation.

She left a note on Chase's secretary's desk telling him that they needed to talk. They needed to get this over with once and for all.

After work, Chase decided to go to the 100 Black Businessmen of Miami mixer that he had been debating whether to attend. He had been a member for the past ten years and found the networking beneficial, but he just wasn't in the mood that night.

Cicely was clearly still avoiding him, because he hadn't seen her at all that day at work. Leonard's confession still had him steaming, and he couldn't believe that Leonard had basically used him as a weapon against the woman he loved.

He knew he couldn't allow Leonard to continue using him to hurt Cicely. He would have to leave Mainstay. Luckily, he was in the right place to get the ball rolling on that.

He turned from the bar area and smiled. He saw just the man who would allow him to land another position and thus clear the way for him to right his wrongs with Cicely. This fellow businessman owned one of the top import/export businesses in Miami, if not the entire country. He'd been trying to get Chase to come into the large Bahamian-based company for years. He'd also been trying to get Chase to meet his sister-in-law for years. Chase wasn't interested in the sister-in-law, but he was interested in the job.

Chase held out his hand in greeting and the two men shook.

"How's it going, Harrington?" Chase said as he shook hands with Carlton Harrington III.

"Things would be going a whole lot better if I could entice you to Harrington Enterprise, Yearwood," Carlton hedged.

"Let's talk," Chase said as they walked away to find a nice corner to negotiate in.

After having secured another job and given his notice to the higher-ups at Mainstay, there was only one thing left for Chase to do…get his woman back.

That Friday morning at Mainstay started like any other morning, with an end-of-the-week meeting in which all of the division heads met with the president of the company to discuss the week's events and plan for the following Monday's all-company meeting.

Being in the same room with Leonard was a chore, but at least he wouldn't have to suffer the fool much longer.

"I have one more thing I'd like to bring up and I hate to bring it up right before the holidays. But something has to be done with Cicely Stevens. She just isn't cutting it in finance." Leonard spoke like it pained him to be throwing Cicely under the bus, but Chase knew differently.

Chase narrowed his eyes at Leonard in warning.

Ron Samuels, the president of the company, cleared his throat. "I know that you've had some concerns about Cicely in the past, Stone, but you haven't said anything in a while, and she was a stellar employee before you came here."

"I know what her record was before I came here, and that's why I have kept her on this long—"

"I think Cicely Stevens needs a more challenging position." Chase cut Leonard off. "Since my position will be open again now that I'll be leaving Mainstay in the New Year, I would think that Cicely should be considered for it."

Ron Samuels nodded. "I wanted Stevens for the promotion, since we usually try to promote from within. But once we found out that we would be able to get a shark like you in the tank, well…" Samuels laughed. "Sorry there just wasn't enough excitement here to keep you motivated, Yearwood. If there was a VP slot open, I might be able to compete with your offer and come up with a counteroffer… But enough of that. I value your opinion, Yearwood. You're a good man. Stevens is definitely my pick for division leader in Mergers and Acquisitions. And since I'm the president, my pick holds weight."

"But, sir, surely—"

This time Samuels cut Leonard off. "There's no need to argue, Stone. You wanted to do something about Stevens, and come the New Year, she'll be out of your division and out of your hair. This meeting is adjourned."

Chase walked out of Samuels's office feeling just two inches shy of vindicated. He clearly needed to have one more conversation with Leonard about Cicely.

But when he walked up on Cicely blasting Leonard off, he began to rethink his original line of thought. Cicely didn't need him to save her. She could very well take care of herself.

* * *

Cicely had known the pencil-wielding maniac was going to break free sooner or later. She tried to coax her back into the cage, but it was too much fun being up in Leonard's face pointing her pencil at him.

He had come back from the division leaders' meeting even more evil than his typically evil self. She had almost thought he was going to stop being such a bear, because he had been somewhat civil the past few days. But no…he was at it again.

So there she stood in front of him, waving her pencil and waging holy hell.

"And another thing," she sneered, "I am not incompetent. You are just impossible to please, and you wouldn't know competent and professional behavior if it smacked you in the face. I am good at my job, and you had better start treating me with some respect or I will file a grievance and I will keep filing grievances until I have your job. Are we clear?"

Leonard didn't say anything. He just glared at her.

She noticed that he was looking behind her, and she hoped that it wasn't another company higher-up. She had tried to keep herself tamed, but the crazy lady inside had had enough.

She turned to find Chase standing there.

Oh, good, the crazy woman with the pencil thought, *the other one.*

She turned to have it out with Chase. She hadn't wanted to do this in the workplace, but since he didn't seem to want to come see her at home as she'd asked him to in the note she left for him days ago, oh, well.…

As she walked over to him, he walked around her and over to Leonard.

"Hey!" *What the hell!*

Cicely spun around and followed Chase.

"I suggest you heed her warning, Leonard. Because if I have to tell you again not to mess with the woman I love, it won't be pretty. Cicely can clearly take care of herself. But just in case I didn't make myself clear enough the other day, my woman is off limits. You harm her or try to harm the woman I love again in any way and I will kick your ass. I might not be working here at Mainstay after the New Year, but trust and believe I will know if you do anything to her. And be clear, I don't make idle threats." Chase spoke his words in an eerily calm voice.

Cicely's eyes were wide with shock. She certainly hadn't seen that coming. Even the crazy, pencil-wielding lady inside of her was quelled. Cicely backed up as Chase turned and started walking away.

"Hey!" She followed behind him.

"You said you don't want to talk about our

relationship at work, so we'll talk later, Cicely. And just so you know, I'm taking another position at another company, so all your little no-fraternizing rules will be null and void." Chase dropped his declarations and kept right on stepping.

She kept right on following. "But I left you a note days ago asking you to come and see me at my condo, and you never showed."

Chase stopped then and stared at her. He seemed to calm down just a little.

"I never got your note," he said. He reached out and touched her face. "We'll talk soon."

And he left.

Cicely stood there dumbstruck until Leonard walked up behind her.

"I took the note you left for him, tore it up and put it in the trash. You may have used his idiotic feelings for you to screw your way into the Mergers and Acquisitions division leader position once he leaves, but you're still a pathetic, sorry little… Ouuuuch! You. Bitch!" Leonard grabbed his thigh in the spot where her pencil had jabbed him.

She looked down at her hand and waited for the moment of regret to come. When it didn't, she just smiled. "It was just a poke in the meatiest part of your thigh. Man up!"

Chapter 14

The entire next week at work she felt like she was moving in slow motion. Chase still hadn't come to see her so that they could talk. And she was beginning to think that she had blown it big-time with him. The pencil to the thigh must have done its job—that and Chase's threats, no doubt—because Leonard had stopped being a jerk for the most part. So that was one saving grace.

Another saving grace was that her brother-in-law, Carlton, had put the fear of God into Isaac when Isaac had shown up at her condo more than a little tipsy begging her to take him back. Latonya, Carlton and the kids had come over to help her decorate her

Christmas tree. They had all decorated Gran's tree the week before, and next they were going to have a big tree-trimming party at Carlton and Latonya's mansion on Millionaires Row in Coconut Grove.

When they were all at her condo, Isaac had shown up and Carlton took a little walk with him. She normally would have felt sorry for Isaac and told Carlton to go easy on him. But she didn't have it in her that day. Her next step was a restraining order. When Carlton came back and told her that Isaac wouldn't be bothering her again, her only response was, "You didn't kill him or anything, right?" When Carlton gave her a funny look and said no, she was cool with whatever he had done and didn't need any more explanation.

Her family's all-consuming holiday preparations kicked into high gear with Christmas right around the corner. Latonya and Gran were making more demands on her time. And even though she was feeling more than a little antisocial, she relished having something to focus on besides the fact that Chase had professed his love for her when he threatened Leonard, and then didn't talk to her about it at all.

So, she took the Christmas shopping trips and the Christmas baking that the two women demanded of her in stride. At least if she kept busy, she thought, she wouldn't have a spare moment to think about Chase.

Business didn't seem to do the trick of making Cicely forget about Chase, though. She told herself that she was a Stevens girl and she was tough enough to handle it. But what did she make of the fact that Chase was leaving Mainstay in the New Year and the job that she wanted, the job that she thought he had stolen, was going to be hers, after all?

She'd believed she had everything under control, but there was the little problem of not being able to sleep because she missed Chase so much.

Miserable and wanting to wallow in it, Cicely was the last person folks should have wanted at any holiday tree-trimming party. She wasn't in the mood to party. But she couldn't very well take another island trip the way she had done the week of Thanksgiving. And somehow the idea of an island getaway without Chase by her side held very little appeal.

She was committed to drinking eggnog and trying to have fun in spite of not having heard from Chase yet. Feeling like a confused Mrs. Scrooge, she gathered the Christmas spirit to go on.

She knew an evening with her niece and nephews would ground her at least for the evening, but what was she going to do with Chase's declaration of love, especially since she hadn't heard from him since then? Could she trust in it and risk her heart for more than a fling? Could she take the chance that what she and Chase had was the real thing?

She rang the doorbell to her sister and brother-in-law's mansion fully expecting their long-time maid, Jillian, to answer the door. But instead, Chase answered the door.

Surprised and also a little giddy, she took a small step back. "Chase? What are you doing at my sister's house?"

Chase grinned his sexy little grin and looked up. She followed his gaze and noticed the mistletoe above the door. He pulled her into his arms and gently coaxed her lips open. He kissed her with a pent-up desire that amazed her.

He pulled his mouth away and inhaled her scent as if he were taking everything into memory. Finally, he took her hand and walked inside, closing the door behind him.

He led her to the downstairs sitting room and kneeled in front of her when she sat down on the antique Queen Anne sofa. He took her hand in his and she felt her heart stop and then start again.

Chase stared at her intently. His gaze had purpose. She held her breath and then let it go nervously about three times before he opened his mouth to speak.

"As it turns out, Cicely, a friend of mine from the 100 Black Businessmen of Miami group that I belong to has been trying to get me to come and work for his family-owned import-export company for years. But I could never give up the thrill of corporate raiding to work importing and exporting petroleum from the Bahamas. When I finally left corporate raiding for a kinder, gentler job, he came at me again wanting me to join his company. This time I took him seriously. And given your no-fraternizing rules…" He slanted his eye at her playfully. "We have to do something about all your rules, by the way…"

She giggled softly and let out the breath she'd been holding, only to start holding it again. If Chase was going where she thought he was going… She exhaled again and then inhaled deeply, holding it until she couldn't any longer, and started the process again and again. It seemed to help a little with her nerves.

"Anyway, given your rules about dating in the workplace, I knew I had to find another job. So I finally told this friend of mine that I would join his company. And he was very happy. But then he started going on and on about this sister-in-law of his that he wanted to try and arrange for me to casually meet so she wouldn't think he was trying to set her up. He had been trying to get me to meet this elusive sister-in-law of his ever since I'd met him years ago, and since I had had no desire to settle down and valued my friendship with this man, I had always respectfully declined. But this time he went on and on about this sister-in-law who was sweet but had some odd obsession with nerds and whose latest loser boyfriend had the nerve to cheat on her. And her story sounded so familiar that I had to ask him what his sister-in-law's name was."

Cicely exhaled then. Her heart burst with so much love and joy it made her stomach ache. She clutched her free hand over her mouth.

"I'd never asked before, and now I'm sorry, because as it turns out his sister-in-law is the woman of my dreams." Chase pulled a ring box out of his pocket.

"Say yes, Aunt Cee Cee, say yes!" Her little niece, Evie, was jumping up and down with glee.

"Shhhh." Latonya placed her finger in front of her mouth to quiet her rambunctious daughter.

Surprised, Cicely looked up. She was shocked to see Carlton and Latonya standing in the sitting room with the little terror Evie and their sons Carlton IV and Terrence. Her grandmother and Jillian were also standing there waiting.

She turned her gaze back to Chase and she let herself believe what she was almost too scared to believe.

Chase opened the ring box and the most beautiful diamond ring she had ever seen was inside. It was a princess-cut diamond with small round diamonds around the band.

She opened her mouth and closed it again. She couldn't speak. She didn't know what to say. She felt a tear coming down her cheek, and Chase wiped it away.

"Now keep in mind, if you say yes, we are going to have to reenact this entire thing for my mom and all the patrons of Margie's Rum Shack."

She nodded and Chase laughed.

"And also keep in mind that if you say yes, you are forever barred from coming up with any rules or ground rules meant to limit my time with you. You'll be stuck with me forever, Cicely."

Cicely closed her eyes and nodded as her heart melted with pure and unmitigated relief and belief.

He said *forever,* and *forever* meant happily ever after.…

"Cicely Stevens, I love you. Will you marry me?"

"Yes, Chase. I love you more than words could ever say. I want to be your wife. I'm *sooo* ready to be your wife."

Chase kissed her then, sweetly and completely.

They then trimmed the tree and took advantage of all the mistletoe hanging in the mansion—that is, whenever Carlton and Latonya weren't taking advantage of it.

And Cicely knew without a doubt that sometimes rivals made the best lovers, and she'd found her paradise in her rival's arms.

* * * * *

They're making power moves that can only lead to one thing...

Lovers Premiere

Essence bestselling author
ADRIANNE BYRD

Limelight Entertainment is Sofia Wellesley's whole life. When she discovers her agency is about to merge with its biggest rival—which is run by her childhood crush-turned-enemy Ram Jordan—she thinks her anger will get the best of her. So why is her traitorous heart clamoring for the man she hates most in the world?

L♥VE IN THE LIMELIGHT
Fantasy, Fame and Fortune...Hollywood-Style!

"Byrd showcases her unique talents with this very touching and memorable tale."
—*RT Book Reviews* on *LOVE TAKES TIME*

Coming the first week of November 2010 wherever books are sold.

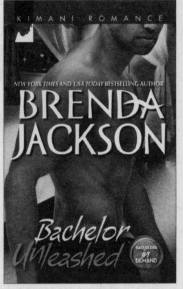